A Slice of Life

By Heidi Butcher

Foreword

I joined the navy at the age of nineteen, but after a couple of years I realised it wasn't the lifestyle for me. I moved to Shropshire with my boyfriend Tim, and after spending months living in a rotting caravan he got a job in Nottinghamshire, so we were off on our travels once again.

This is the story of how I conquered my weight battle, love battle and heart-over-mind battle.

Chapter one: Rock bottom

I felt as though I had lost all my self-esteem after leaving the navy. Part of me had died, including the faith I had previously had in myself. I seemed to have lost touch with the nineteen-year-old who had jumped on a train and joined up. I had turned into an anxious, overweight, *Jeremy Kyle*-watching recluse. I felt like a slob.

With no job, I often felt completely hopeless as I stared out over the duck pond our caravan overlooked. It was an idyllic location, but after months of staring out at the same scene day in, day out, it slowly started to become claustrophobic.

While Tim was working shifts at a hotel gym, I would get up very early as the ducks landed noisily on the roof of the caravan. It was made of steel and I think the ducks got confused between the top of the van and the pond! I would hear them land, give out a few miffed quacks and then fly off again with a long take-off run that made it sound as though a herd of elephants was running across the roof.

This was my usual wake-up call and, without a job or any prospects of finding one, life was incredibly frustrating. I was only twenty-three and had hoped the couple of years I had served in the navy would help to land me a job. But unfortunately, experience in radar operating and missile launching wasn't really what employers were after.

My daily routine was to walk into the village, pick up the local paper so I could look for jobs and buy whatever food I could afford. It really was a dire situation. The rent on the van was only fifty pounds per month, but Tim was on minimum wage and I had no money coming in. We seemed to live on pasta and tomatoes, but somehow we managed and we were happy.

We even managed the odd takeaway and wine night, or if we had no money our treat would be a mountain of crisps. Unfortunately, this only led to me becoming larger and larger as I was in the van all day long. I had no transport, no friends and no money. Added to a sheer lack of motivation, this was a bad combination.

The caravan site was home to another seventeen vans, but they were holiday homes, and in the winter no one stayed in them because it was too cold. We used to wake up freezing cold with frost on top of the blanket. We had to go to bed fully clothed – including our hats – under a duvet and two blankets just to try and stay warm.

The van was seventeen years old and had no heating apart from a gas fire in the front room, so we were basically camping. At twenty-three, this wasn't really a problem. We had both just come out of the navy, which must have toughened us up because we never moaned about it or let it get us down. This was the life we had chosen, so we just sucked it up.

In the summer, life was divine; it was like being on a super-long holiday. I used to feed the ducks, sunbathe and grow vegetables. I found that if I planted sprouting potatoes they grew into many more potatoes, and the same applied with carrots and onions. I found growing our own vegetables therapeutic and loved being outdoors. The pond, which was about thirty metres in length and width, provided a lovely backdrop. With a little island of trees in the middle, where the ducks gathered, I had myself a very noisy party!

Our neighbours were nice. I got on really well with the young couple to our left as the woman was in a similar position to me. Her partner was at work all day and she was at home. But then, one day, they left without a word, never to be seen again, which was all a bit strange. I realised people often lived on these sites because they were in dire circumstances, so I knew better than to ask too many questions.

The funniest thing about living in the van was the bathroom, as the floor was completely rotten. The toilet pivoted on the joists and rocked when you sat on it, and there was a hole next to the sink that gave us a view of the ducks drinking from the water that leaked from the pipes.

My parents came and see us every now and again, but it was a six-hour round trip from Lincolnshire to Shropshire. They were mortified when they saw how we were living and my dad always tried to fix things, as Tim was useless at DIY. They always gave us money when they visited. Without that, I have no idea how we would have survived. They even gave me money to buy a car so I could get to interviews. I used it to a buy twenty-five-year-old Renault 12, which I proudly called Reg. He was long, gold and slick, with gorgeous steel bumpers that curved around the front of the car.

I had never owned a car and, like everyone else, it was only after I started driving it that I really learnt to drive! The beautiful bumpers got bashed into walls, posts and anything else I couldn't quite see as I was reversing or parking. However, this newfound freedom didn't last long. I constantly had to be towed back by Geoff, the caravan site owner, as I ran out of petrol on numerous occasions because I couldn't afford to fill up the tank.

After twelve months of this lifestyle, I was three stone heavier. I was almost ready to move back to Lincolnshire to live with my parents, as no jobs were coming my way and Tim's job wasn't going anywhere. But then Tim got a letter to say he had been offered a job in the prison service in Nottinghamshire. This was the best news ever. Tim was slightly older than me and had taken redundancy from the navy, so he had eight years of service under his belt, which had thankfully paid off.

'So, Bella, let's get packing and leave this dump behind,' he said when he heard the news.

Tim's blue eyes suddenly had their sparkle back and he started to stand tall again. Six-feet-plus tall, to be precise. After living the way we had for two years, we were both shadows of our former selves. I certainly didn't feel like a twenty-three-year-old. I probably resembled a fifty-plus-year-old on the verge of menopause. At least Tim had finally found us a life away from the van and the ducks.

'This is it! This is what we've been waiting for! I can't wait... So where's Nottingham?' I found myself saying.

I had heard of the city and had seen the advert for Tunes cough sweets, where a man tries to buy a ticket to Nottingham but can't pronounce it because of his blocked nose, but I wasn't sure where it was. I was happy just to wait and see. To be honest, I didn't really care. I was just relieved not to have to go cap in hand to my parents after another life failure.

When I left the navy, it felt as though I had let the Queen down when I told my mum it wasn't for me. Even to this day, the navy isn't discussed at home. It's like that part of my life never happened; as if it were an unfortunate blip. We have never had a conversation about the reasoning behind my life-changing decision to quit the job I had wanted to do since I was nine years old.

I suppose one day I'll sit them both down and tell them the cold, hard truth about the toughest couple of years of my life, when I contemplated suicide but was fortunately saved by a pub!

As I looked down over the cliffs near the navy training camp, I had been plucking up the courage to throw myself over and put an end to the bullying. But over my right shoulder, about a mile away through the sea fret, a pub had appeared. It was as if it was beckoning to me, saying, 'Come in, sit down and think about it.'

I'm so glad I did. One day, when the time is right, I'll tell my folks all about it.

Chapter 2: A new life beckons

Each armed with a suitcase, and with a week to go before Tim's course started, we were on our way to Nottinghamshire. It was only an hour away from the caravan site, but it might as well have been on the other side of the world as we didn't know anyone there. One massive bonus was that I would be closer to my family, but not too close. It was just close enough for Dad to drive there and back in a day without causing my mum's brain to explode with his extreme road rage.

Tim was driving our clapped-out Audi estate, which his parents had given us. It was originally set to be taken for scrap, so we had sort of inherited it, but it got us from A to B and had been getting Tim to work for the previous few months. I was slightly worried that it wouldn't get us all the way to

Nottingham, but hey ho, we would get there somehow!

I had been forced to leave Reg behind. Although I loved that car, it was old and quirky, and definitely wouldn't have got us to Nottingham without us putting about two hundred pounds of petrol in it and topping it up with water every ten miles. Geoff had taken a liking to the car and said he would look after it for me and use it around the site. To be honest, Geoff had been so kind in terms of towing me back whenever my car had broken down, and giving me lifts here, there and everywhere when I needed to go a little further than the nearest village, so I was happy to leave Reg with him.

As we left, I looked back at our caravan. I felt extremely sad, as it had been my home for many months and I felt as though I was leaving it behind to be lonely, sad and cold all by itself, but Geoff had told me that it was falling to bits and would be towed off for scrap. I thought it was charming that he had finally realised what a heap of junk we had been living in through freezing cold temperatures!

I waved goodbye to Geoff and the ducks, and never looked back.

As I grabbed hold of Tim's hand, I felt excited and nervous.

'Let's go and start our new life,' I said. 'Did you sort out somewhere for us to live?'

'Well, sort of,' Tim said with a sheepish look.

I knew that meant no. 'Do you mean sort of yes or sort of no?' I probed.

'Well, the thing is, I've been really busy at work and the boss has been hanging around, so I couldn't use the phone to ring any rental companies and...' his explanation tailed off.

'For God's sake, Tim! So for the last week you've known we were moving and haven't sorted anywhere for us to live?! I haven't had a phone or any means of doing it, so I was relying on you. We've just left our home, which is probably being towed away as we speak, and we've got nowhere to live!'

'Something will crop up,' he assured me. 'We'll just have a drive around when we get there and look for "to let" signs.' He looked at me with a little smirk on his face and gave a cheeky thumbs-up.

'OK, have you got a map?' I asked. I was determined to have a look at Nottinghamshire and see if anything jumped out at me.

'Yeah, I think my dad kept one in the glove box, unless he took it out.'

I reached over to open the glove box and there was still an A-Z in there, which surprised me as his dad was quite tight and usually claimed everything he could. I decided he must have forgotten it was in there.

Looking at the map helped a lot... not! It was just like every other city, with a busy centre surrounded by suburbs and villages.

We were heading for the north of Nottinghamshire, towards the prison where Tim would be working. It was near a village called Bradbury, which was ten miles or so away from the centre, or at least that's what I deduced from looking at the map. I suggested that we head there as a starting point.

I noticed as we travelled that everywhere was very green and flat. There were miles of flat fields with either wheat or corn crops growing in them. I think I must have been a farmer in a past life, as I loved being in the countryside. Even though I grew up in the suburbs of Lincoln, I have always gravitated towards the sea or green fields. I had never really been a city girl, but then I had never tried it, so I was willing to give anything a go.

We blasted past a sign that read 'Welcome to Bradbury'.

'Slow down!' I hollered. How are we meant to look for a place if everything's a blur? Forty-five isn't the new thirty, you know!'

Tim slowed right down to a pathetic crawl.

'So funny, aren't you?' I responded. 'Keep your eyes peeled. We need something before the end of the day end or we'll end up in a B&B and we can't really afford that.'

I liked Bradbury right from the start. It was quaint and green; everywhere I looked, from people's front gardens to the roadside, I saw well-kept trees, shrubs and flowerbeds. There was a church and a little parade of shops, which had the usual greengrocer's, butcher's and baker's shops, and of course a small supermarket, which was always handy.

There weren't many places available to let or for sale, and I was starting to think that even if we had found a place we wouldn't have been able to afford it. I began to feel a little apprehensive as I loved the place, but I was worried that the small amount of money we had wouldn't stretch far enough.

We were nearing the edge of the village when we came across a static caravan park called Sunnyside with a 'To let' sign outside. This had to be fate, I decided.

'Tim! Pull in here! Look, vans!' I was so excited I couldn't get my words out quickly enough.

'Really, Bella? I thought we'd left that way of life behind us.' Tim couldn't hide his disappointment.

'But that's probably all we can afford, and it'll do until we find our feet. Pleeeaaaase?' I begged, giving him my best puppy dog look.

'OK, but it's only temporary.'

'Yeah, fine. Just pull in before you miss the entrance,' I replied, grinning from ear to ear. I was thrilled that we had found somewhere to live so quickly, and that it would be a kind of home away from home.

We pulled up into the car park near the site office and I jumped out.

'I'll see if they have anything for us,' I shouted as I approached the office, which was nothing more than a glorified shed.

I walked in to a tinkle of chimes and a lady who I can only describe as eccentric beyond words. Judging by the way she was dressed, she was very much into her knitting. She was adorned from head to toe in the stuff. It was a little chilly out, but it still seemed excessive.

'Morning, can I help?' she asked in a posh voice with no hint of an accent. She sounded very chipper.

'Yes please. I was wondering if you had any vans to let, as we saw the sign outside.' Hope was abundantly present in my voice.

'Oh, I'm sorry. That sign should have been taken down weeks ago, I keep forgetting. But I can take your number in case one comes up,' she said, smiling.

I was unable to hide my disappointment. 'Oh really? Oh no... Oh noooo.' For some reason I started to cry. I had felt as though this place would be our salvation, only to be told there was no room at the inn.

'Oh my word! Sorry, my darling. I'm sure something will come up, though.' She gestured me over for a hug.

Then suddenly she turned around and started scrabbling around on the wall behind her. I could see various numbers and hooks, which I assumed were van numbers and key hooks. Right at the bottom was a single key without a tag. The lady grabbed it.

'Look, I do have one van. I don't usually rent it out as it's for my son, who's traveling around Asia at the moment, but you can stay in it for now as he isn't back for another six months. It's lived in, but I'm sure it'll be better than nothing... Would you like to take a look?' she asked with a kind smile.

'Yes please!' I replied. My tears soon dried up and were replaced by a huge smile.

I ran outside and shouted to Tim: 'Come on! We have somewhere to live!'

Then I remembered I hadn't asked how much it would cost. 'Erm, excuse me, sorry. I forgot to ask how much it is.'

'First, please call me Fran, and second, the van is forty pounds a week, which includes all your bills. Is that OK?' Fran looked at me sheepishly, as if she was waiting for me to say that it was too much.

'That's brilliant, thank you!' I replied.

It was less than we had been paying and Tim would be earning more. Things were getting better and better.

As Tim got out of the Audi, the car door squeaked and it sounded as if he had let one go. I let out a little giggle. It may be childish, but trumping still makes me laugh.

'So let's go and get you settled in,' said Fran cheerily.

We followed her through the caravan park. It was so cute, with vans hidden among the trees and shrubs and her eccentric touches everywhere, from chimes to hanging candleholders.

'Nearly there,' she called, as we had fallen slightly behind.

'Looks lovely, doesn't it, Tim? We've really fallen on our feet here!'

Tim grabbed me, gave me a big squeeze and kissed the top of my head. He had to bend down to kiss me as he was so tall and I was only five foot two. We always looked a bit odd when we walked anywhere together.

'Right, here we go,' Fran said. She opened up a curtain of weeping willow and there it was.

'A campervan?!' we both said in unison.

'It's not just a campervan,' Fran shared. On the other side is a huge awning and a hot tub!' She waved us over to take a look around.

The van was bright green with a white stripe. It wasn't in bad nick and it wasn't that old, but the size was a problem. We couldn't possibly live here... could we?

Round the back was a huge awning, which could be completely closed off to the elements. Inside was a table and chair set, along with a heater and fridge, which looked unused. I stepped inside and it was very cosy. At least, cosy is a much nicer way of describing it than small! But I liked it anyway. I liked the location, I liked Fran and I liked the feel of it.

'Tim? Tim?' I called, but he was nowhere to be seen.

I ran back to the car to find Tim in the driver's seat with the engine running. He was fuming. I opened the door.

'Come on, let's get the cases out,' I said, ignoring his bad mood. I pulled mine out of the boot and the lid slammed down, nearly trapping my fingers.

'I'm sorry, Bella, but there's no way I'm staying there. It's too small, too cramped and too weird. Sorry, but we can find a B&B for tonight and have another look tomorrow. This is just the first place we've found; there'll be plenty more. Just get in and let's go.' He didn't even look at me as he spoke.

'But I love it! It'll be OK till we find somewhere bigger, and for forty quid a week it's a bargain, eh?' I tried to sound cheerful, but I felt as though something had changed between us the moment we had walked through that willow.

'There's a reason it's only forty quid, you know! Come on, Bella, use your brain. How on earth are we both meant to fit in there with my height and your weight?' He pointed his finger at me angrily.

I had never seen this side to Tim before, and he was acting so mean. I knew I had put on weight; it had been creeping up and up without me really thinking about it. But it had obviously been on his mind. We hadn't seen a great deal of each other while we were living in the van as Tim had always been out working or training, as he was a fitness fanatic, so nothing had really been discussed as I had nothing exciting to say. We had simply sat and watched telly whenever we were together.

'That's not very nice. I know I'm slightly larger, but I'm still the same person. I've moved my whole life to be with you. So what if I've put a few pounds on? That's 'cause I was rotting away in a cold, mouldy caravan trying to find work without a phone or reliable transport. I had no friends or family, and no help from you. And now you decide it's a problem after I've agreed to move so you can further your ambitions!'

By this point I think I was slavering and slightly red-faced, not having paused to take a breath.

'Annabel, I haven't once asked you to do anything. You've just followed me around like a lap dog. Do you really think I wanted to live in that depilated old caravan and work my arse off to pay for it? Do you know how many times my mum told me to move back in with her and dad without you?'

He still wasn't looking at me, which was starting to piss me off. The information about his mum was new, but I could imagine her saying that as she had never been my biggest fan and always mentioned my weight whenever she saw me.

'So what do you suggest? Should I just get in, shut up and let YOU drive us around till YOU find us a place to live?'

'What I suggest, Annabel, is that you go home to Lincolnshire, get yourself a job and stop living this stupid pipe dream that everything will be OK. It isn't OK. I'm done with all this crap. All I want is bricks and mortar, a job, and some money for a nice car and a holiday.' He was looking straight at me. 'Sorry, Annabel, but I'm done. We want different things.'

With those words ringing around in my head like the birds in cartoons when a character is dazed, I took a step back. Without hesitation, I screeched, 'Go!'

He shut the door without saying another word and drove away. He indicated left at the end of the driveway and then he was gone.

Chapter 3: Moving on

At that moment, Fran appeared out of the shadows. 'Is everything OK, darling?' she asked kindly.

She had obviously heard what had just happened. I could tell by her tone.

'No, everything isn't OK. I'm stuck here with no money, no job, no transport and no man!' I sat on the floor and sobbed.

What else was there to do?

'Come on, darling. Let's make you a cup of tea and have a little chat.' Fran had such a kindness in her voice it was impossible not to get up and follow her lead.

We made our way to the office and Fran put the kettle on. 'Sit down, my love. What's your name, by the way? I haven't actually asked you that yet.'

'It's Annabel, but people call me Bell or Bella.' I couldn't hide the despair in my voice.

'Well I think Annabel is a beautiful name, so we'll stick to that around here. Do you feel you can tell me what happened and why your young man made such a sharp exit? I know the van isn't five-star, but I didn't think it would send anyone running for the hills.'

Fran was giving humour her best shot, but at that moment all I wanted was a hug from my mum, not someone I had only known for half an hour; the half an hour in which my world had fallen apart. But I needed to unload and I had no one else to talk to.

'Thanks, Fran, and I'm really sorry for bringing this to your door. I'll be on my way shortly, as I have no way of paying you for the van. I'd be really grateful if you'd let me use your phone. I'll call my folks and ask for a lift to Lincolnshire. It'll make their day, but it feels like so many backward steps for me.'

I looked down at the floor. I would rather it swallowed me up than have to go home. I felt defeated. Having spent so many months in a caravan that was falling down around our ears, I had come to Nottinghamshire to start a new life, only to find I had been dumped. The thought of going back to my old life was mortifying. It was as if I had done it all for nothing. I felt so stupid for rejecting my parents' help all that time and pretending everything was fine when it was obvious to everyone that we weren't fine, and that the situation was anything but fine.

'Well of course you can use the phone, but can I offer you a suggestion? I'm looking for someone to clean the vans, maintain the gardens and generally help me around the site. If you're interested, I'll let you stay here rent-free and you'll get an extra seventy pounds a week to do whatever you like with. Have a think about it, and if going home is still a better prospect, I certainly won't be offended.'

With a glint in her eye and a turn of her back, the world suddenly unswallowed me and told me to pull myself together.

'Are you sure you're not just feeling sorry for me?'

Fran interrupted. 'Darling, gift horse and mouth. Are you with me?'

'Yes please. That sounds great. Can I just get my head around the situation for a day or so before I start? And I'll need to ring my folks. Is the offer of using the phone still available?'

'Of course! Use it whenever you want. Just don't be calling your Great-Aunt Audrey in Australia,' she said with a twinkly smile.

So there I was in Bradbury without transport, money or a familiar face. But I had a job and a home, which was more than many people my age had. Most of my school mates were still living with their parents, undertaking never-ending college or university courses.

It had only been an hour or so since Tim had left, and it seemed life was giving me an ace in one hand and a joker in the other. I figured it was how I played my hand that would count.

I felt the best thing to do was ring the folks: firstly to tell them I had arrived safely in the dodgy Audi, and secondly to tell them that Tim had left.

Somehow, I knew I would never see him again, partly because I didn't know where he had gone, but also because I felt quite glad and free that a tough and emotional decision had been made for me after we had coasted for the best part of a year.

Things hadn't been as exciting as they had when we were in the navy. Living together and seeing each other – or at least breathing the same air – every day had taken its toll. I think we had just grown out of one another. As Tim had quite rightly said, we wanted different things. It was time to find out what I truly wanted; to start living life for myself and not for someone else.

I sat down on the swivel chair at the makeshift office desk and rang my mum's number. It just rang and rang and rang.

'Oh, come on! For God's sake, pick up!' I bellowed down the receiver.

My mum had a habit of leaving the phone a little too long sometimes and then it automatically went to answerphone. She never picked it up after one, two or three rings, just in case people thought she was sitting by the phone waiting for it to ring. She usually picked up after the fifth ring, which drove me bonkers because I knew she was in!

'Hello?' she answered in a breathless voice.

'Hi Mum, it's Bella. You OK? You sound puffed out.'

'Yeah, I'm fine. Just had to rush to get the phone before it went to answerphone.'

I nearly asked if it kicked in on the sixth ring, but held my tongue.

'Oh, OK. Glad you're all right. Dad OK?' I asked, trying to make small talk.

'Yes, I think he's as well as Dad can be, you know, with his hip and knees and heart, but he's been gardening today, trying to get it all ready for the spring. Oh, and he put a bird box up. He thinks we might get some sparrows.'

'Erm, Mum,' I interrupted before I lost my bottle. 'So you know I moved to Nottinghamshire?' I continued hesitantly.

'Yes, how did it go? Did the Audi make it?'

'Yes, but, erm, me and Tim didn't.'

'Oh heck. Did you have to get towed back?' Mum's tone had instantly changed to sympathy.

'No, I mean Tim and I are, well, no more. We... *he* called it a day, said it wasn't going to work...' I started talking really fast, but the words weren't making much sense.

'That's a shame. Although I never liked him, anyway.'

'Mum! What do you mean? You can't say that! Why tell me this now?'

'Well, he was never any good for you, to be honest. He left you in that rotting caravan day and night while he was God knows where.'

'He was at work...'

'Well, so he told you. I didn't trust him, though. There was something shifty about him... So where are you? Are you coming home?' Her tone had suddenly become very matter of fact, as if the deal was done.

'No, I'm not actually. It's all a bit weird really. We made it to a caravan site and I ended up with a job and a home and no boyfriend, all in one day.'

Hearing myself say that made me wonder whether I was thinking straight.

'Whereabouts? Do you want Dad to come and get you?' A note of genuine concern was apparent in Mum's tone.

'No, Mum, honestly. I'm OK and it's the first job I've been offered in months, so I think I'll stick it out. My new boss said I can use the phone any time, so I'll be in touch tomorrow with the address and phone number. Is that OK?'

'As long as you're sure, Annabel. You really are best rid of Tim. He never did you any favours. I'll tell Dad the news, but phone us tomorrow, OK?'

'I will, I promise. And thanks, Mum. Love you.'

'Love you too.'

It wasn't often I heard my mum say that, so it left me a little emotional. The whole situation felt draining, but I knew I needed to get on with it or I would end up in an even bigger pickle.

I walked back to the van park entrance to find Fran, but she was nowhere to be seen. All I wanted to do was unpack my case and try to make the campervan feel more like home.

'Fran! Fran! Helllooo?'

Bloomin' 'eck, I thought.

I started to make my way towards the campervan, trying to remember how to get there. Luckily, it was a nice day; not too cold, just a nice spring day. I could hear the birds twittering away to each other in the trees and bushes, and every now and again I spied a caravan among the bushes. They were all green statics, and most had decking around the front and sides. They looked really cosy and well looked after. Fran obviously had an eye for good tenants.

I could tell they all cared about presentation, as they all had lovely flowerbeds or newly laid white gravel. All of them looked really quaint, except one, which stuck out like a sore thumb. It was an older van, stuck in a corner by itself. I started to wonder whether anyone lived in it as the grass wasn't cut and there were no flowerbeds to be seen.

But as I looked more closely, I could feel someone watching me. I started to walk towards my new van, but the shadow behind the window disappeared.

It could have just been my imagination, I thought. *I couldn't see Fran letting one of the vans get so neglected without saying something.*

It was time to go and find my new home.

'Annabel, is that you?' It was Fran.

'Yeah, it's me. Where are you?' I responded.

'Just turn to your left and come through the weeping willow. I'm just giving your van some fresh air. It's been a while!' Her words echoed through the trees.

'OK, I'll come and find you!' I headed to the left and stumbled across the weeping willow. I crept through the hanging branches and there she was: my new home. I felt really attached to this little place already, even though it was only the second time I had clapped eyes on the van.

'Right, Annabel, here are the keys. Make yourself at home. I've put you some basic supplies in, but I think a little shopping trip in the morning will be needed to keep you going for more than a day or so.'

She handed me thirty pounds in crumpled notes.

'Call it an advance,' she said with a smile. If you need me, I live in the van right in the corner with the unkempt grass. You can't miss it.'

She said this with a knowing smile. She had obviously seen me gawping at it earlier.

Chapter 4: A happy home

My suitcase was already in the van. I had left it by the entrance before Tim legged it, so Fran must have wheeled it round. I popped my head through the door and looked left and then right, taking in the sights and the smells. It smelt a little musty, with a hint of weed. I figured Fran's son obviously liked the odd smoke or two.

I decided to give it a good clean the next day as it was a little 'lived in', but I knew I could get it all shipshape and tidy. Fran said she had put clean bedding on for me while I was on the phone to Mum, but I still shoved my head into the duvet and sniffed it to see if it was clean. She had been true to her word and I was relieved. I wouldn't have been able to sleep in a smelly boy's bed.

The decor was a mixture of Fran and a masculine version of Fran, with wind chimes and scented candles thrown in. There was a pile of books on the sideboard next to the sofa bed. The books were mostly about tropical and backpacking destinations, but the one that leapt out at me was a large, red, hardback with big black writing that read: *The desire of the mind meets the desire of the body.*

I wonder why that caught my eye!

Then I turned my attention to making the place look and feel like home. To the left was a seated area, which turned into a bed, and to the right was a bench with a collapsible table, which did the job. Along from the seated area was a kind of kitchen. It had a tiny sink, hob, chopping area and microwave, which was all I needed. I loved a ping-ping dinner. In the corner near the driving area was a wardrobe and a couple of tiny drawers, which would just about fit my smalls.

Outside in the awning was a fridge-freezer, the picnic table and matching chairs, and a heater. Luxury!

The curtains were black, which I didn't think was in keeping with the feel of the van, although it was a good way to keep the sun out in the early morning. I decided I would change them as they made the van look a bit like a meth lab.

I grabbed my suitcase and started to unpack. I felt a little sad and it started to dawn on me what had happened.

Can I really do this? I asked myself.

I had taken a job from someone I didn't know and was living in a van on a site I couldn't have pinpointed on a map, bit it was either that or go back to my folks. So, with a heavy heart and a lot of determination, I started to make the van my home.

When I had packed my suitcase, I hadn't really taken much notice of what I was putting inside, but as I unpacked I realised it actually told the story of the two years since I had left the navy and moved into the caravan. When I had first met Tim, I was a size ten. I was almost twenty-two and very active at the time. I had loved running and most other sports I was asked to play. Plus being in the navy had made it easy to keep fit. There hadn't been much else to do socially while we were at sea.

I pulled out some size twelve jeans, which looked tiny, but I remembered them from our first winter in the van, when I had been at my happiest. The caravan had been exciting, as it had been my first real home with my man. I had finally been independent from my parents and the navy. We had lived from day to day, and from hand to mouth, but we were in love and we weren't bothered. We hadn't needed anything but one another.

Then I picked up a size fourteen pair of shorts. I had worn them the first summer after we had been living in the van for six months or so. Having lived on rubbish food and crisps as a treat on Friday nights, without taking any exercise, I had gone up two sizes in as many seasons.

A tear rolled down my left cheek as I remembered this as the turning point in our relationship. This was the time when I had started to see less and less of

Tim. He had been working more and more, and had kept telling me he needed to as I wasn't earning. Even on minimum wage, his full-time salary should have covered the rent and more.

What had he been doing with his money? Why had he always been skint?

Then I picked up some new shorts I had bought in the spring, as the others hadn't fitted any more. I had gone up to a size sixteen, and at five foot two I realised this wasn't the way I wanted to be. My legs chafed together at the top and my T-shirts revealed more than just a muffin top.

Why would Tim have wanted to stay with me in a campervan when he was a walking advert for Better Health *magazine?*

I wanted to make out that he was shallow, but deep down I knew it was primarily my own doing. I had been happy just cruising along, making myself think this was what happiness was and to be grateful, when all the time I was alone and probably the unhappiest I had ever been.

Why hadn't Tim been there in the evenings? Where had he been? And why had he suddenly left me without flinching? Why, why, why?

It was as if someone had just whispered the answer into my ear. It was obvious he was having an affair!

Oh my God, he was having an affair, I thought to myself. *Course he was.*

It all suddenly made sense: the late nights, the double shifts and the overtime with no money to show for it.

How could I have been so stupid? How could I have let it happen? How on earth had I not seen it and realised?

I sat on the bed and wept and wept. All the signs had been there and I really felt like a fool.

How could all that time have gone by, having left all my ambitions and self-worth behind just to help someone else use me to better himself?

That's exactly what Tim had done. He had found a new job with good money. And here I was living in a campervan, earning seventy pounds a week.

But I still had my dignity. I would bounce back and start my own life.

***

I woke the next morning with a start and a feeling of not knowing where I was. All I could hear was the sound of a song thrush. Sunlight was shining in through the van's sunroof.

Hmmmm, they forgot the blackout curtains for that, didn't they? I thought to myself.

I wasn't sure what time it was as I couldn't find my watch. As I peeped through the curtains, I guessed it was about seven. If I was right, that would constitute a massive lie-in for me as the damn ducks had landed on the roof at around five every morning when we had lived in the old van.

I was really hungry and thirsty, as I hadn't had anything to eat or drink since lunchtime the day before. I was also dying for a wee, but unfortunately the camper didn't have a toilet. The nearest facilities were located in the shower and toilet block. I was still dressed in the clothes I had worn the previous day, so I would have to hotfoot it to the toilets before I peed my pants.

After a quite an emotional evening, I somehow felt cleansed of all my troubles and woes as I made my way there. It was a new day and it provided the clean slate I had been looking for. I needed to erase Tim from my thoughts and start living for me; to start considering myself and what I wanted.

Where's the flipping toilet? I really am going to pee my pants at this rate! I thought to myself.

'Morning, darling. Sleep well?' a voice called from nowhere visible.

'Eh? Oh Fran, it's you! You gave me a fright. Sorry to be really rude, but I'm desperate for the loo. Where is it, please?' I was starting to do a little jig and holding my bits as subtly as possible.

'Right in front of you, darling,' Fran said, pointing to a bush.

'Really? Do I have to pee in a bush? I thought there might be a toilet block or something?' I wasn't hiding my impatience well.

'Yes, the entrance to the toilet is behind the bush,' Fran responded with a giggle.

'Brill!' I shouted as I shot off quicker than a bullet from a gun.

To my great surprise, the toilets were out of this world. It felt as though I had just walked into a five-star hotel with its marble floor entrance. In front of me was a door marked 'Toilet' and to my right was a door marked 'Shower'. As I was desperate for the loo, I ran through the first door, swinging it open.

Oh, the relief as I released my bladder. It was better than sex!

Well if felt like it to me, but it had been a while.

There was a white porcelain sink with Molton Brown hand wash and hand cream lined up against gorgeous turquoise and cream mosaic tiles. It was like a hotel en suite. Once I had washed my hands, I looked into the shower room to find a walk-in shower with a huge, round shower head and a glass screen. It was immaculate, as if it had never been touched. I was relieved, as I would be using the toilet and shower regularly, not to mention cleaning them.

I came out of the block to find Fran waiting for me. It was starting to get warmer and sunnier.

'Do you fancy some food and coffee, Annabel? I think after yesterday you deserve a little rest.' She put her arm around me.

Fran was slightly taller than me, and I guessed she was in her early fifties. She had greying, curly, wild hair, which she held back with multiple grips and scrunchies. But she seemed to pull it off; she really did have style, albeit a unique style. She was wearing a long, navy, flowing skirt with a simple, oversized orange vest top and a knitted cream cardigan. This sounds horrendous, but somehow it just worked.

I was glad to see that she had gone a little easier on the knitwear, though. I usually hated stylish people, as I couldn't put an outfit together for toffee, but I got the feeling Fran wasn't trying hard to be stylish; it just happened for her. Some people just know what goes together.

I tended to think, *Yeah, looking good*, and then see a picture of myself later on and think, *Really? What was I thinking? I look so fat and frumpy!*

'Yes please, that sounds great. Can I just grab a shower in the poshest shower block I've ever seen?' I bowed and gestured towards the block with my arm.

'Ha ha, you're funny. They have just been done, to be honest. But no one else uses them, as everyone has a shower and toilet in their van, so I think you may just have them to yourself.'

'Oh, I hope so. They're gorgeous. It makes me feel like I'm in a five-star hotel instead of a house on wheels.' I winked at Fran, hoping she wasn't offended by that last comment.

'No problem. The chickens have laid some eggs this morning and I have some sausages, so hurry over when you're finished at the Hilton!' A huge smile broke across her flawless, happy face.

'OK, will do.'

I ran back to the van to get my towel and toiletries. I felt like I needed a good scrub, so I could literally 'wash that man right out of my hair'. It was probably all in my mind, but I could still smell him. It felt like he was lingering on my skin and in my hair.

I enjoyed a slower walk back to the shower block, taking a good look around the place as I did so. I was still getting my bearings. I loved how all the vans looked as though they were lost in the woods, as every now and again one popped up from nowhere. Luckily, it was only a short walk from my van, so I hopped straight into the shower. I couldn't believe how good it felt to get into a proper shower after washing in our old van, which had felt like showering under the overflow of a sewage tank.

I got a little carried away and started singing 'You're Beautiful' by James Blunt at the top of my voice, completely forgetting where I was.

'Erm, excuse me. Erm, hello miss!' There was a man standing in my shower room. He had his eyes clamped shut and was handing me my towel.

'Argh! What the fuck? What the... What on earth? Get out!' I was trying to cover my ample beasts and other parts. I wasn't sure which bits I wanted to cover most. I grabbed the towel and wrapped it around me as quickly as I could.

'What's going on? Why are you in here, George?' Fran was pushing George out of the door, apologising to me as she did so.

Flipping brilliant! I thought. *I find a great place to have some 'me time', only to be perved on by some loon called frigging George. Great!*

Fran came running back in.

'Great,' I said. 'I might as well put a sign on the door saying, "Everyone come on in. I'm naked and love to be watched in the shower!"'

'Sorry about that. It was George, our oldest and longest-standing resident. He means no harm. He lost his wife earlier this year and I think it's changed him. I'm not sure, but I think he might be starting to suffer a bit of dementia. Anyway, make sure you lock the door in future, just in case he has a little walkabout.'

'Yes, I will. Bless him, I hope I didn't startle him too much. It was just a bit of a shock having someone looking at me while I was in the shower, albeit with his eyes shut!'

I smiled and started to giggle.

It was quite funny, to be fair. Poor George would be having nightmares for life after seeing me naked and more than a little unkempt in the lady garden area.

'I think I'll have to call his son, as he needs more care than I can give. I'm not a carer, I just care.' She shrugged and looked a little defeated.

'I think that's probably for the best. He obviously needs a little more attention than you can give him. Anyway, are the sausages cooked? I'm starving!'

'Yes, nearly ready. Just follow the smell of fresh coffee and sausages,' she said, floating off with a smile.

I made my way back to the van with only my towel wrapped round me.

Blow it, I thought.

It was a tad cold, so I quickly got dressed, walked through the weeping willow curtain and headed towards Fran's overgrown grass and unloved van.

I spotted Fran out on the decking. She had cooked the sausages on the barbecue as well as frying the eggs in a pan on the top stove. She was holding a jug of coffee and held it out to see whether I wanted a cup, so I gave her the thumbs up.

'It feels so much better having fresh clothes, hair and skin. The food smells lovely. Thanks for doing this, I'm starving,' I said as I plonked myself down in a wicker chair. It was so comfy and I loved the way the wicker scrunched noisily when I moved.

'Bet you are, darling. It's nearly lunchtime! I bet you haven't eaten anything since yesterday, have you?'

'Is it really? I thought it was about eight or nine o'clock! Time flies around here, doesn't it?'

I mentally wrote a note to myself. I needed to find my watch so I could enter the real world again.

'One egg or two?'

'Two please. Diet starts tomorrow!' I joked.

It really should have started years earlier. But hey! What's an egg or two between me and my boss? I thought.

Chapter 5: Back to work

After a very lazy day, Fran suggested a bottle of wine to round off the evening as my new site maintenance job would start the following morning. I was really in the mood for some wine. I felt like a bit of a charity case as I still had no money apart from the thirty pounds Fran had given me for shopping, so everything I was eating and drinking was donated, which went against the grain for me.

I made my way over to Fran's van again. I could hear her talking to someone, but I could only hear my new employer's voice. She was speaking in a higher pitch than usual and sounded a little irrational.

'OK, fine. Best pack up and get back then. Why did I spend all that money on a round-the-world ticket when you're only using it for one flight?!'

There was a pause as the person at the other end of the phone line spoke.

'So about a month, then? OK, well keep me informed of what you're doing and take care, Justin. Don't get into any more trouble while you're there, OK?'

There was another pause and I felt a bit awkward as I was loitering outside, listening in to her conversation.

'Yes, OK. Bye, sunshine, love you too. See you in a month or so.' Fran's tone had softened a little.

I knew if I entered then it would have been obvious I had been listening, but my desire for a glass of wine was more powerful than my conscience at that moment in time.

I walked onto the decking, which needed a good scrub, as I nearly fell onto my bottom with every slippery step. I knocked lightly on the door and it flew open before I could finish my standard knocking routine, which usually consisted of two knocks, a pause and then another knock.

'Evening, Annabel. Have you had a good afternoon? Hope you've made yourself at home and got your bearings.' Fran sounded as breezy as ever.

She didn't mention the phone call, so I pretended I hadn't heard a thing.

'I've actually had a lovely day, I just chilled out. I hope you don't mind, but I moved the camper around a little bit; just bits and bobs to make it feel more like home. I've also managed to fit all my clothes in.'

'That's lovely, and you do whatever you want with the camper, as long as you don't drive it away,' she said.

A smirk appeared on her face, but I got the feeling she meant it.

I laughed, but I took the hint. I was just a staff member and a guest, after all.

'No chance of that, Fran. Anyway, when do you want me to start and what do you want me to do?'

I was hoping she would tell me to take the following day off so we could hit the wine hard!

'If you could start tomorrow, that'll be great. The Joneses' caravan needs cleaning as they're coming over this weekend to open it up. It's quite early in the season, as most of them do that in May time, but I guess end of April is a good time to make the most of the season. They've had a bit of trouble with their eldest son, Lucas, who you'll probably meet at the weekend.'

'OK, no problem. Where is it, and where do you keep the cleaning stuff?'

'I'll show you where everything's kept and on the way I'll point out the Joneses' place.'

She started walking away and gestured for me to follow her, so I did.

We were nearly at the entrance by the time Fran pointed out the Joneses' van. It was a cute little unit, probably with two bedrooms, but it had all the same neat touches as the others. Fran was obviously doing a great job of looking after the gardens. Although the van had been uninhabited since late the previous year, the grass had been cut regularly and flowers were popping their heads out of the ground towards the sun.

Fran popped her head into a little cupboard behind the office. It contained all the cleaning and gardening equipment. It was well stocked with every kind of cleaning product on the market. She either liked cleaning or simply enjoyed buying the products. I wasn't quite sure which, having been in her van. But the rest of the site and the toilets told a different story.

We headed back to her van for a well-deserved bottle of wine on the decking, then I headed back to my camper to get an early night ahead of my first day at work.

***

Fran had given me a key to the Joneses' place, so I hotfooted it over there the following morning to make a start. Inside it was the cutest van, with two bedrooms, as I had thought, and a shower room. The dining area flowed into the lounge and kitchen. It was all newish and well looked after; a complete revelation having previously lived in such a rundown caravan, which had really only been fit for the scrapyard.

I spotted some photo frames perched on the side. One contained a family photo of the Joneses. They had two boys, who were both gorgeous but looked very different. The taller of the two had mid-length blond hair with a little kink and a sun-kissed glow. He had a pretty, almost feminine face, but a square, manly jaw. The smaller Jones boy had short, blond hair and a similar face, although it was a little more intense. It looked as though he needed a long holiday to chill out with his older brother.

I got lost in the cleaning as I had found my MP3 player and was listening to The Killers, my favourite band at the time. Before I knew it, I was finished. I took a good look around and was pleased with my work, although I felt quite envious that someone else would be sleeping there at the weekend.

I headed back to the office to find Fran, but as I had anticipated she was nowhere to be found. I put the cleaning box back in the cupboard and wandered over to her van.

'Fran, hello?'

There was no reply. I was a bit stuck for what to do next. I didn't want her to think I had packed in work for the day. I wondered whether I should start doing a bit of gardening or cutting the grass.

I sat on her decking, picking at the long grass that was growing through the boards. After about half an hour I decided a shower and change of clothes were in order, as I had been sweating like a pig while I cleaned the hot van. As it was nearly May, it was quite a nice temperature outside, but it was boiling inside the caravans.

I got my washbag together and had a lovely, cool shower in the luxury of my own shower unit, which was carefully locked this time. I had barely had time to think about Tim, but I did wonder what he was doing, where he was, whether he had started at the prison and whether he was enjoying it. I couldn't help but think fondly of him, as he had been my best friend and lover for a long time.

I knew in a way that he had done me a favour in leaving, because I had just been following him around. Maybe I would have done that forever and never done anything for myself. This had made me step up and make my own decisions for the first time in my life, and I quite liked the decisions I had made so far. I knew it was only the first week, but hey... baby steps and all that.

I realised I was talking to myself in my head as I ventured back towards my camper for a snooze. I opened the weeping willow curtain to find Fran sitting on a seat in the awning.

'Oh God, Fran. You gave me a right fright!' I stood there, half-holding my chest as if I were having a mini heart attack.

'Sorry, darling, I've been looking for you and couldn't find you anywhere. I did pop my head into the Joneses' van and it looks and smells amazing. Well done.' She was sitting cross-legged and as still as a statue.

'I hope you didn't think I'd just cleared off for the day. I couldn't find you and I wasn't sure what to do next. Do you want me to start on the grass or weeding?'

'Don't worry about it. Just take your time and make your own rota. As long as everything gets done, I'm happy. I just came over to give you some money, as I thought you might be needing some. An advance of a week's wages would be appropriate, wouldn't you say?'

'That would be great, Fran, and very kind. I feel like a little sponger at the moment, but I'd love to go and stock up the fridge and overhead cupboards, as I've been living off what you've fed me and crisps so far, and that's a habit I want to ditch.' I felt a bit self-conscious as I realised eating crisps instead of meals was really a backwards step, and I was determined to do something about it.

'Annabel, after a few months working here, you'll soon snap back into shape, believe me.' She walked over to hand me an envelope with the money in.

'Right, dinner's at seven, hope you like curry. You can bring a bottle of red,' she said, tipping her eyes in the direction of the envelope.

'Oh, are you sure? You really don't have to.'

'I know. See you at seven, then.' And with that she disappeared beyond the willow.

Chapter 6: Making new friends

I decided to wander down into the village, as I hadn't had time to have a look around up to this point. The walk was a little less than three-quarters of a mile and it was a gorgeous afternoon. The birds were singing, the flowers were in their final budding stage, dying to meet the sun, and aeroplane tracks had been painted across the pale blue sky, taking lucky holidaymakers to gorgeous beach resorts full of sunshine and cocktails. That was something I was longing for... a holiday, not a cocktail.

I couldn't remember the last time I had taken a holiday. I guess some might have thought my year in the caravan was one massive holiday as I wasn't working at the time. Some might question why I would even need a holiday. But it was the whole booking process, getting excited about the trip, buying new clothes or a new novel I couldn't wait to read and being waited on hand and foot without having to cook, clean or think that made me jealous. I figured I needed to sort out my present situation before I started dreaming about jetting off somewhere. That and the fact that I was skint.

Ah well. Back in the village of Bradbury, a market was being held in the little village square. It looked like a second-hand market offering old trinkets. One lady had a knitwear stall, and I got the feeling this was where Fran had inherited her unusual dress sense from.

I went over to the knitwear stall and had a browse for something I could give Fran as she had been so kind to me.

'Hi there, love. What can I do you for?' asked a gorgeous-looking lady from among the knitted cardies.

'Oh, hi! Didn't see you there. I'm looking for a, well, I'm not sure. It's for a friend, well my boss, kind of. You see?'

I was running the garments through my fingers, wondering what Fran would like best.

'I see, and where do you work?'

'At Sunnyside, the static caravan site down the road,' I said, pointing along the road in case she wasn't sure where it was.

'Oh right! I take it your "boss" is *Fran*, then,' she said. She had suddenly started to speak in a totally different, and quite abrupt, manner.

'Yes, that's her. She's been really kind to me and I wanted to buy her a gift to say thank you.'

'Well, I'd watch your back, young lady. Looks can be deceiving, I wouldn't trust her as far as I could throw her, and as for that son of hers, Justin, he needs a firm hand. He may be in his mid-twenties, but he thinks he rules the roost... and the village for that matter. I was glad when he got sent packing by Katy Jenkins' dad after Justin got her pregnant, but he wasted no time whatsoever getting cosy with her best friend. I don't know... there's no discipline nowadays. Anyway, just watch your back. You're living in a viper's den.' With that, she descended back into her knitting as if I wasn't there.

I headed towards the local express supermarket, sharing pleasantries with the locals as I went: a nod here, a hello and good morning there. It was all very nice, but I could tell there was some restraint. It felt as if they were checking me out.

I got what I needed from the express: mainly wine, bread, milk and coffee. I was determined that no crisps or bread would pass my lips, at least for a while. To be honest, I was sick of the sight of them. I topped the rest of my basket up with rice, noodles, pasta, pesto and Shreddies. I had always loved Shreddies, and I gathered they were healthyish. That would do me for the time being. I could always nip back if I ran out of anything.

As I bimbled back to the site, the knitwear lady's words were swirling around in my head. I wasn't sure how to take what she had said.

Was she just a bitter and twisted old gossip? Or was there some truth to her accusations?

I wasn't too sure I liked the idea of living in a 'viper's nest', but I decided to make a conscious effort to forget what she had said. After all, Fran had been nothing but charitable towards me and I had no reason to think anything other than kind thoughts about her.

Before I knew it, I was back at the site. It had taken me no time at all to walk back, but my arms were killing from the weight of the bags and I was glad to get back and put them down. I enjoyed filling up the cupboards with the groceries I had bought.

I had a quick look at the time and realised it was nearly time for dinner. Time at the caravan site seemed to just disappear; sometimes a little too fast. I quickly changed, although I wasn't too fussed about what I wore, and I didn't have many options. I was only having dinner with Fran, after all.

As I wandered over to her van, I heard several voices inside. They were all chatting away and sounded very animated.

I gently tapped on the van door and gave a quick hello.

The door swung open and it was Fran. 'Well hello, Annabel. How are you, darling? Have you had a good day?' She was rather over-affectionate and I was quite taken aback by her hugs and kisses.

'Erm, fine thanks... You OK?'

'Yes, fine. Come in, come in,' she said, ushering me in with a massive smile on her face.

I stood rooted to the spot with unfamiliar faces staring at me. They were all seated with either a beer or a glass of wine in hand. I felt like time had frozen and I was part of a play that had been due to start half an hour earlier. It looked as though they were still waiting for a performance.

'Hi,' I said. A little shy smile was all I could muster.

It was then that I saw a face that stuck out from the rest. He looked about my age, and was handsome, with a ginger-tinged beard, sun-bleached, shoulder-length locks and a huge smile that shone through the mist of my shyness. I tried, but I couldn't take my eyes off him.

'These are the Joneses. They arrived earlier than expected because Lucas got an earlier flight back from Dallas after visiting his gramps and grandma.' Fran looked more than welcoming as she told me about the strangers in her van.

'Oh right, the Joneses. Hi there. I hope the van was clean and well looked after when you got in there?' I knew I looked uncomfortable and fidgety, but there was nothing I could do about it.

'It sure was, thank you,' said an extremely glamorous lady with a thick Southern American accent. 'It was nice to come back to. We can be sure to have a nice quiet time now we're here. It's been nonstop for the last forty-eight hours, with airport pickups and then travelling here from Wigan.'

I was transfixed by her gorgeous accent. It wasn't often that I heard a different accent, especially such a distinct American drawl.

'Wow, all the way from Wigan, hey? And there was me thinking you were from the States.' I gave a gentle smile, unsure as to whether my attempt at humour would be lost on them.

'I like her, Fran. She's got a sense of humour and she's cheeky with it!' Mrs Jones returned my smile.

She was very well groomed. Perfect hair, check. Manicured nails, check. Matching handbag and shoes, check. And a huge diamond ring.

That would have involved a huge cheque! I thought.

My eyes kept wandering over to Lucas, and I felt as though his eyes hadn't moved away from me either. But that couldn't be right. I decided I was probably just being paranoid. Or maybe it was wishful thinking.

Mr Jones simply sat there without saying a word. He looked older than his wife, but that was probably because he wasn't as fussed about looking after himself. He had a little pot belly, a double chin and a nondescript expression on his face. The travelling had probably done him in; he looked ready for bed.

'If you guys can come to the table, dinner's ready,' Fran said, ushering us into the 'dining area', which looked very snug for five adults. It contained a small, round table which could drop to become a bed. It felt even more snug as I was rubbing shoulders with people I had literally just met and didn't know the first names of, apart from Lucas.

'So, hi. Erm, my name's Annabel and I just started working here a couple of days ago.' I thought that was the best I could do in terms of an introduction without making it sound as though we were all in rehab.

'Well, howdy Annabel. My name's Jude and this is my husband Lucas, and my son Lucas Junior.' Jude grabbed my hand with one hand and my wrist with the other, giving both a tender squeeze.

Lucas Senior remained silent, while his son smiled and waved hello.

'So, do I call you Junior or Lucas? Or Lucas Junior?' I was trying not to sound too controversial, as I didn't know if there was some sort of etiquette involved.

'Call me Lou. Most of my friends call me Lou and my dad usually gets called Lucas,' Lou said with a strong Wigan accent. This took me aback slightly, as I had been expecting a southern drawl to come out. I felt a bit tricked by my imagination and let out a giggle.

'Hey, what's so funny?' Lou asked, giving me a little nudge.

'Sorry, I wasn't expecting you to be so northern.' I started to giggle more at his accent for no fathomable reason.

'Eh, what's up with a good old Lancashire accent?' Lucas Senior had stopped inspecting the cutlery and had spoken with an equally strong accent.

'Oh, nothing at all. I think it's gorgeous. I just wasn't expecting it after hearing Jude speak!'

'Oh, I still find it hilarious, honey, and I've been listening to it for over twenty-five years.' Jude gave me a little wink.

'Lou's older brother Zachary is very much a cowboy. He lives over in Texas, running the business for Lucas. He said he might come over this summer, but he says that every year.' Jude looked down at her feet. She was obviously upset by her son's absence.

'Where are you from?' I asked in an attempt to steer the conversation away from Zachary.

'Dallas, born and bred. I go back as often as I can, seeing as my folks are still there and all my family, and obviously, Zachary. But this little sweetheart here wouldn't leave his godforsaken Wigan or Wigan Wanderers, so I had to move my ass over here.'

She grabbed her husband's cheeks, something he was obviously used to as he gazed up at the ceiling without saying a word.

'Right then, who's hungry?' Fran asked. She was busy getting a dish out of the oven and I normally would have offered to help, but there was no space.

'I'm starving,' I responded. I really was, as I had hardly eaten.

'I bet you are, love,' piped up Lucas. It was only the second time he had spoken and I wasn't quite sure what he meant by it.

Was he suggesting I was hungry because of my size or because I had been grafting on their van? Or was he being suggestive?

We were all given a plate of lasagne with salad on the side, and it was delicious. We all enjoyed a glass of the red wine I had chosen from the supermarket and I couldn't have chosen better, even if I had known what it would be going with. I'm sure on the back it had said that it would go well with quiche! Thankfully, I had bought two bottles or the wine wouldn't have stretched very far.

There wasn't much small talk during the meal. We were all hungry and ready for some food. After we had finished, Jude offered to wash up, which took me by surprise as her manicured hands looked as though they had never washed a single dish. Fran thanked her but insisted on leaving it until the morning.

'Right then, ladies,' Jude said. 'I'm bushed and I need to hit the hay. Even just travelling from Wigan has done me in. Lucas, are you ready for bed?'

'Yes, petal. You should try driving from Wigan, that's even more tiring!' He gave me a cheeky grin. He was quite attractive for an older man, despite the pot belly and double chin. I could see where Lou got his looks from.

'I'll come too. The flight over wasn't the best and I need some shuteye before tomorrow.'

'I may as well walk with you, if that's OK?" I aimed the question at Jude, as I didn't want to look like a desperado.

'Sure, hun,' she replied.

She grabbed my arm and we were out of there.

'Night, Fran. Thanks so much for the dinner. See you tomorrow for a catch-up and a gossip. I need to find out how that son of yours is doing!' Jude drawled on the way out.

'Night all, thanks for popping over. See you about eight, Annabel. Lots to do!' She waved us off and locked up behind us.

I had forgotten about the job. I would have to be up with the lark to start. Oh well, it's always better with than without, and eight was still a lie-in compared with life in the old caravan.

Chapter 7: A secret liaison

I woke up feeling really refreshed. A decent meal and a single glass of wine had been just what I needed, rather than the snacks and bottles of wine I had been consuming over the past two years.

I had set my alarm for seven thirty and was quite happy just to roll out of the bed, get a quick wash and dress.

I took a slow wander over to Fran's the next morning. I loved the early mornings at the site. All I could hear was birds singing, the odd car passing on the main road that ran alongside the park and very little else. That particular morning was a little cool for the end of May; there was still a nip in the air.

As I approached Fran's van, I did a double take. When I looked back, I saw Lou making a quick exit and giving Fran a brief backwards glance as she watched him from the main side window.

Surely not? I thought. *I mean, she's old enough to be his mother or possibly even his grandmother.*

I stopped in my tracks and jumped behind a bush. I didn't want her to see me, but seeing as I was due to arrive at eight I wondered if she had planned it so I would see them together.

Sod it, it's not me who's sleeping with someone young enough to be my son, I thought.

I marched up to Fran's van and knocked on the door. She eventually answered.

'Oh, morning! Everything OK, Annabel?' She looked a little confused and dishevelled.

'Morning, Fran. You told me to be here for eight, ready for work?'

'Well yes, but it's only five to seven. I was still in bed! Maybe come back in an hour when I've had a shower, hey?'

'Oops, sorry! I forgot to change my watch! See you in an hour.'

I slunk off feeling a tad embarrassed, even more so because I had seen something I shouldn't have. I knew then that it was obviously a secret. And I hate keeping secrets; even secrets I shouldn't know.

Since I had an hour to kill, I thought a nice long shower was in order. I hoped it would wash everything I had seen down the plughole; if I had actually seen anything, that is.

I was still enjoying the fact that I still had the shower room to myself and access to the nice products Fran had supplied. I quickly dressed after my shower because, before I knew it, it was nearly time to meet Fran.

'Morning!'

I quickly turned to see Luscious Lou standing half-naked with just a towel protecting his modesty.

'Hope you've left me some hot water.' He performed mock hand guns, adding to my concern that his towel might slip.

'Hi, erm, yes. It's lovely and warm.'

'Cool, I'm so ready for this.'

Lou closed the door to 'my' shower room behind him. I was sure his towel would be on the floor in no time.

Stop it, Annabel! Stop it!

I continued my walk over to Fran's van, past all the saplings and budding flowers. Apart from having to share my shower, life had improved considerably and was I was so glad I hadn't given in and moved back to live with my parents.

They were already back to discussing the mundane facts of life when I phoned, for example how many hard drives my dad had added to his computer and the badminton class my mum was obsessed with. I was doing my best to sweep the whole Tim situation under the carpet. I still thought about him, but it was what it was, and I was determined to make the best out of a bad situation.

'Hi, how's you again this morning?' Fran said, grinning at me.

'A bit cleaner. I managed to get a quick shower,' I replied as I started walking up the steps to her van.

'Turn yourself around, my girl. We have some gardening and major weeding to do today and for the rest of the week. This sunny, moist weather has sent the weeds into overgrow!'

'No problem. Where's the gardening stuff? Is it with the other bits and bobs in the shed near the office?'

'No, they're here next to my van.'

I followed Fran round to the other side of the van to find a huge lock-up shed. She was busy unlocking it, and when she opened the door it was like tool city.

'Right, darling. Grab yourself a tool or two of choice and let's get to it.'

Fran grabbed a hoe and passed me a fork, spade and rake.

This was hardly a choice if you asked me, but hey, it was gardening and these seemed to be the best tools for the job in hand.

'First, we need to go to the Whites' van and give their garden a spruce up, as they're arriving at the weekend. Then we need to do the McKenzies', as they're also arriving at the weekend. Then I'll leave you to it and you can do the Joneses'.'

My ears pricked up when she mentioned the Joneses, carefully looking for a reaction from Fran that would give her secret away, but there was nothing.

Boy, she has a good poker face, I thought.

We got stuck in and passed the time with short conversations and grunts as we worked on the ground. I loved this job. It was physical and out in the fresh air, and the sunlight was getting warmer and longer by the day. It was heading towards June which was always a great month for me as it made me feel as though we were heading towards the summer.

This lifestyle was already agreeing with me. I was feeling physically fitter, which always made me feel and look better, and I was starting to lose weight without even trying or noticing. The only way I knew was that my jeans were literally falling down. They were my fat day jeans, not even my fatter day jeans, so I was really pleased.

I suppose I had stretched them slightly with all the movement, but hey, a loss is a loss and a win's a win in my book. A few more weeks of this and I'll be Vogue *material*, I thought.

It was funny how I could make myself giggle just by having little conversations in my head. This was probably due to the many days and nights I had sat by myself in the caravan with nothing but my own mind and the telly for entertainment.

Before I knew it, Fran had put down her tools and shouted, 'Time for a brew, darling.'

I sat on the bench in front of the Whites' van. It was a cute white bench with gnomes either side.

'Hey, sweetie, how y'all doin' this beautiful mornin'?' Jude shouted from the other side of the trees. I couldn't see her for all the willows, but I recognised the accent right away.

God only knew how she could see me. She must have had tree vision or something.

'Fine thanks, Jude. Enjoying the sunshine,' I shouted in the direction of her voice.

Then suddenly she appeared from behind the trees. She looked stunning as she pulled them to one side and clambered through. She had a bandana wrapped around the top of her head in a big bow and was dressed in linen trousers and a pink shirt, with a long beige cardie over the top to take the morning chill off. She looked so out of place. She would have been more at home on a cruise liner than on some caravan site for the odds and sods brigade in the middle of rural Nottinghamshire.

'Oh, you look so funny sitting there among the gnomes. You look like the ham in a gnome sandwich.' She pointed to the gnomes to emphasise her point.

'Hahaha! Hey, just call me gnome meat!'

I laughed at this as I thought it was funny, and thankfully Jude was either being polite or found me funny because she joined in.

'Do you know where Fran is? I need a quick with word with her,' she said a little more soberly.

Had she found out about Lou and Fran's liaison the night before? I wondered.

I debated whether I should tell her where she was or pretend I didn't know, but it was a small van park and she knew where Fran lived, so she would soon catch up with her. I wasn't supposed to know anything anyway, so I pretended nothing was amiss.

'She's taking five in her van and making us a brew. I think that's where you'll find her.'

God, snitching is so much easier, I thought to myself.

The last twenty-four hours had definitely been the most eventful since I had arrived, mainly because there had only been me, Fran, George, and the odd comings and goings of people opening up their vans until this point.

I hoped I hadn't dropped Fran in it, but I couldn't see why I shouldn't tell Jude where she was. With that, I heard 'That's your last warning' in Jude's raised voice, followed by a door slamming loudly.

Fran turned up with cups of tea and a smile five minutes later. 'Here we go, darling. Help yourself.'

'Jude popped by looking for you earlier. Did she find you?' I asked. I could tell that I was blushing at my own tactless question.

'No. I'm sure if she needs me she'll keep trying.' Fran looked away and changed the subject by drawing attention to a rhododendron growing within the white flowerbeds.

Chapter 8: Settling in for summer

The weeks flew by and we found ourselves slap bang in the middle of summer, and it was a hot one. I was well into the day-to-day life at Sunnyside. We mainly lived at an easy pace, but some days were really hard work, especially when I dug up the gardens to make way for new flowerbeds or for decking. But the exercise was doing me no end of good and the weight was still dropping off.

I got to meet most of the residents and it was a mixed bag of city people, mostly from the Birmingham and Nottingham areas, but some from as far as London, Wales, Yorkshire and Scotland. I found it fascinating that they chose to keep a holiday home on this particular site. It certainly wouldn't have been the first place I would have thought of if I was choosing a second home. I had always had Cornwall and The Lakes in my top five places to live, having spent many happy holidays in both areas with my folks.

However, I had fallen in love with Bradbury, and it was a simple life. The people were eccentric and loved a gossip, it just had that small village gossip vibe I hadn't ventured any further afield as I hadn't needed to so far. Bradbury had everything covered.

Having spoken to some of the people renting on the site, I gathered that people mainly chose this place for a sense of escapism and to rest after their stressful weeks at work. This was especially true for the families with young children. I really didn't envy their lifestyles: getting up at five to get the kids to pre-school clubs at seven, racing to work before the rush hour started and then doing it all again in reverse.

I felt like saying, 'Just move here!' But that was the whole point. If they didn't work so hard they wouldn't have been able to afford the double lifestyle. Fortunately, they always looked chilled when they came to stay and the kids loved it.

George had been placed in a home by his son, which was a shame, but it was a decision that had needed to be made. George's son had a heavy heart about it, as he felt he should have been caring for his father himself, but he realised this was a massive task and that he would have had to leave his well-paid job to care for him, which would have had massive implications on his family.

We had a little leaving party for George, but we weren't sure if he enjoyed it as he kept doing his disappearing act.

The Joneses hadn't been seen since the day I had heard Jude having words with Fran. I had asked Fran whether they were due to return any time soon. I knew it had only been a couple of weeks, but I had been under the impression they would be around a lot. I was very disappointed not to have seen Lou. Even though he was having a bit with Fran, it was nice to have some eye candy around the place.

As I was mainly outside all day, apart from when I was doing a bit of DIY on the vans, I was starting to get a nice tan and was feeling a lot healthier. That was mostly due to a much better diet. Crisps were an 'every now and again' treat, rather than a meal consisting of about five bags. This meant I was losing weight. I had no idea how much, but even my normal jeans were falling off me. I was starting to feel as though I looked my age again and less like a frump.

Tim had done me more favours than I could ever have contemplated. While I still found myself thinking about him and wondering if he was getting on OK at his new job, I didn't have even the slightest inkling to go and find him. It was more like the sense of hope I would feel if I had a brother who was enjoying his new job.

I had made a few changes to my abode, turning it into more of a chick's den than a hippy retreat. I had got rid of all the scented candles and wind chimes and put strewn them around the grounds surrounding the van. I had put some voile up to make it look cosy and softer, thrown some cheap throws over the benches and put a PVC covering over the makeshift table. It was all about adding something of my personality to make it feel like a proper home.

Since Lou had gone, I was back to having the shower room all to myself again, apart from the odd time the plumbing went haywire and the residents had to use the site's facilities. Life was so sweet and it was becoming my saving grace. Finally, I was doing something with my life. OK, so I was really just a caretaker on a caravan site, but it was so much more than I had been only three months earlier. I felt like I had been there for years, like I fitted into an Annabel-sized slot, which was thankfully a little smaller now.

Chapter 9: The return of the Joneses

I woke up late and I could see the sun shining in through the sunroof. I had tried to put some blackout material over it, but the daylight still shone through around the sides. I wasn't too bothered about getting up as it was my day off, which was nice as it had fallen on a Friday. As we were up to date with all the vans and gardens, Fran had given me four days off in a row.

I lay in bed for ages, just thinking and listening to the songbirds. That was the only negative thing about campervans and caravans: every sound was amplified. But over the previous year or so I had become accustomed to it, I even needed a little noise to be able to sleep.

As I lay there, I could hear a familiar accent. It was Jude. I recognised her voice immediately as it was so unique around these parts. It sounded as though she was outside talking to someone whose van was about twenty-five metres from mine as the crow flies. I could generally hear whatever was going on in that sort of circumference around the van.

I thought about getting dressed, but I couldn't be bothered. I had wanted to see Jude, Lucas and Lou as they had left so quickly, but now they were back I decided it could wait.

'Hello, sweetie. Are you there?'

It was Jude and she was staring in through every window to see if she could spot me. I held the covers tightly over me, as I always slept naked.

'Oh, hi Jude. Erm, can you give me a minute? I'll pop over when I'm dressed, if that's OK? Just give me five!' I shouted towards the door.

'Sure thing, sweetie. I'll put some coffee on.' And with that she was gone.

I said 'so long' to a nice lie-in and 'hello' to having to get up and dressed earlier than I had wanted to on my day off.

Oh well, it was nice that she had come to find me, I reasoned.

It would be good to have a proper chat with someone, as I hadn't really had much communication with anyone. Even Fran had been preoccupied and was on the phone in the office a lot of the time. I never asked why, but I guessed her son might have had something to do with her subdued mood.

I got myself out of bed and pulled some denim shorts on. I had just bought them from the village charity shop and was amazed to be buying a smallish size fourteen. I was also quite surprised that the village charity shop had them, but I was amazed by the variety of items it sold.

I took a slow wander over to the shower block to use the loo and brush my teeth. On the way, I stroked the leaves on the bushes and ducked my head under the low-lying branches. I had disappeared into my own world and completely forgotten I was meant to be heading over to Jude's.

It didn't help that I opened the shower block and bumped into a naked Lou!

'Oh, I'm so sorry. Erm, I'll go! Sorry Lou!' I was flustered and held my hands over my eyes. I was trying to move in the direction of the door, but instead I carried on walking forward towards him.

'Oops! I don't think that's the door handle you have hold of, Annabel.'

I opened my eyes to find my hand on Lou's penis and to see him standing there all smug, with his hands clasped behind his head, his chest puffed out.

'Aarrghhh, sorry!' I shook my hand away and clumsily opened the door. Then I stood against the wall, trying to catch my breath.

Had that really just happened in my shower block?

I started to relax and then a chuckle broke out.

Why on earth was he so hard? Was he having a sneaky wank in my shower? Ewww gross!

The door to the shower room opened and Lou popped his head around it.

'Sorry about that, I got a bit excited about having a beautiful woman in my naked company. It's been a long time,' he said with a wink before walking off. 'Oh, Mum mentioned you were coming over for coffee, I'll look forward to seeing you. Loving the new look, by the way!'

I turned bright red. I hadn't really thought much about my look. All the mirrors on the site were tiny and positioned at head height, so I hadn't really noticed how I looked from the neck down.

I brushed my teeth and used the loo, and I was finally ready to go for coffee. I had managed to teach myself how to do some cute corn plaits to keep my hair out of the way while I worked. I had noticed my hair was turning a sun-bleached blonde just on the top.

I had always loved my hair. It fell just past my shoulders but was thick and straight, so it was manageable and could be easily plaited. But I was also loving the beach bum look and it was actually on trend at that moment. I regularly picked up magazines from the local newsagent and discovered I was very en vogue for the summer of 1998.

'Come on, Annabel, we're waiting for you, sweetie!' Jude bellowed over to me. Lou had obviously told her he had seen me over at the shower block.

Before I knew it, I could see them. I burst into a huge smile. It was nice to see the three of them again, even though I had only met them fleetingly before.

'Hi everyone. How was the trip from Wigan?' I found a seat and sat down.

'Oh, it was a lot smoother than last time. Having more sleep the night before always helps,' Lucas piped up with a full sentence or two for a change.

'Oh good, glad to hear it. How long are you here for?'

I kept my attention focused on Lucas, but Jude answered. 'We're here for the whole summer. Lou starts a new job in London this September, so we've decided to spend some time together as a family. It's been a rough year with multiple visits to Texas, Lucas' health scares and, well... lots of other things. She gazed over at Lou and then straight back at me.

'Oh, lovely. It'll be great to have you around. What are your plans for today?'

'Do you fancy a ride out, Annabel? We know a gorgeous pub down near the river. It does lovely food and we could feed the ducks.'

Lou looked really animated as he spoke, but all I could think was, *Great, more ducks!*

'Sounds lovely,' I said.

'Here's your coffee. I hope you like it strong,' Jude said, passing me a white cup with a star on it. I took a sip and nearly spat it back out. It was like drinking tar!

'Have you got a tad more milk and sugar, please, Jude?' I must have sounded like a right coffee pussy.

'Course, sweetie. I still make stateside coffee.' She giggled and took my coffee to make it more Brit-friendly.

'When will you be ready to go, Annabel? Shall we say about eleven?' Lou asked, looking at his watch.

'Yes, great. What time is it now?'

'It's just gone ten.'

'Oh right, great. My watch isn't working properly, so I tend to work out the time of day from the sun at the moment.' I pointed up at the sun, just in case no one else knew where it was.

The Joneses' van was very mixed in style. It was kind of like a mock ranch, and it wouldn't have looked out of place in the middle of Texas. I still felt Jude was out of her natural habitat at Sunnyside, but she must have been happy enough to have been coming back for twenty-five years. That would have been a huge lump of her life to have simply been making do.

I quickly drank my coffee, more to be polite than for pleasure. 'Right, I'm going to freshen up. I'll be ready in about an hour.'

'Hey, you look just fine as you are,' Lou said, grabbing my arm as I passed and stroking it.

If I hadn't been wrong so many times before, I would have been sure Lucas was coming on to me. If his past form was anything to go by, he didn't have a set type. But I was enjoying the attention. It was nice to feel wanted again, even if it was only for a split second or the result of a token gesture.

Chapter 10: An almost perfect day

I rushed back to my van to get changed. I was in quandary about what to wear, as I wasn't sure whether to go laddish or more feminine, given the attention Lucas had been giving me. Then there was the other dilemma of finding something that still fitted. Since Tim had left me I had shrunk. I was no longer a sixteen or even a fourteen, I was more of a twelve, as all the smaller size fourteen garments I had were falling off me.

I wasn't sure how much I weighed as I didn't have any scales, but clothes provided the best measurement and I was really chuffed to be back down to a size twelve. I was looking better, fitter and brighter, and my skin was clearing up, probably due to the lack of saturated fats since I had stopped stuffing my face with them.

It was a gorgeous summer's day outside and it was already warm. I decided to wear a summer dress I had worn the previous year. It was a size sixteen, but I wrapped a belt around the waist and hitched it up a bit.

Voila, I thought to myself.

To be fair, I probably looked a right state as I didn't have a mirror, but looking down I felt it was passable, and luckily all my gorgeous sandals still fitted. I had a weakness for flip-flops and sandals, so I had plenty to choose from, and I decided on a pale pink pair with bows on the front. They looked very sweet and feminine, so I decided the feminine look was a go!

Why not? I thought. *Even if I'd read the signs wrong, who cares? I dressed in overalls and boots every day, so it was nice to dress up a little.*

By the time I had faffed about with various outfits, the van looked as if I had been robbed and time had started to tick by.

'Hey, you ready yet?' Lou asked, popping his head in. He had one hand resting on door and was looking at his watch. He looked even more handsome than the first time I had seen him. There was something about the surf dude look that I liked.

'Erm, yeah. I'll be right with you. I wasn't sure what to wear; not much fits any more.' I looked down at the clothes that were strewn all over the van.

'You look great. Let's go, love.'

He grabbed my hand and we strolled off hand in hand, which felt bizarre and a little overfamiliar. I wasn't sure I was comfortable with it, but then he suddenly let go, as if he had read my thoughts.

'Right, let's swing by our van and I'll pick up the picnic.'

'Wow, you've made a picnic! I was assuming we'd stop for a pub lunch or nip into the supermarket.' I was really impressed.

'Hello sweetie. Have a good day!' chirped Jude as she handed Lou a picnic box.

'My mom loves preparing picnics, so it would be rude not to make the most of her enthusiasm.' He smirked cheekily and shrugged his shoulders.

We headed towards the canal, which had a path alongside it that ran for miles. Pretty footpaths led away from it towards other little villages and into the fields. I had only been down there a few times, as on my days of I tended to relax in my van with a book or enjoy sitting out in the sun. I loved this time of year. The flowers were out in force and the birds were singing. It was a perfect day.

And somehow the man in my company was the type of hottie who wouldn't have given me a second look a year earlier. Tim was hot, but in a clean, boring way. Lou was hot in a raw, rugged, 'let's do it now' kind of way. I must admit, my dreams had been overtaken with these images and more.

'Shall we keep walking, or do you fancy eating now?' he asked.

'We've only walked a hundred yards. You can't be hungry yet, surely?' I guess there was an undertone of sarcasm in my voice, which I was trying to tone down.

'Well, if you hadn't taken so long making yourself look beautiful we might have got a bit further by now, eh Bella?' He gave me a sly wink.

I spotted a path with a sign saying 'Jeffers Farm 100 yards'. I knew Jeffers had a duck pond, and I figured that would be the perfect place for a picnic.

'Shall we go up there? There's a lovely duck pond and we can set up camp there if you like?'

'Sounds like a plan. Lead the way.' He swept his arm towards the path for me to lead the way. He looked so cute with his three-quarter-length trousers, flip-flops and campervan T-shirt.

I wasn't too sure about the 'I love Texas' peaked cap, but hey, I suppose he was half Yank.

I started walking towards the duck pond, trying to avoid the piles of dog poo. It always made me angry to see that, as it only takes a second to pick it up. People with dogs must just totally look away and pretend their dog wasn't going to the toilet.

With the duck pond in sight, it took me back to my own private duck pond on the old caravan site, and the beloved ducks that had woken me up each morning with a quack and a flip before they hit the water.

I looked around, but Lou was nowhere to be seen.

'Lou? Lucas? Lou?'

I was a tad surprised not to be able to see him. I turned back around to face the duck pond.

'Boooooo!' Lou shouted as he jumped out of a bush. He thought it was hilarious.

Without thinking, I hit him around the waist. 'Loser! You frightened me to death!' I yelled.

I was actually a little cross, but then he showed me his bottom and ran off.

'Come and get me, Bella Wella!' he called as he shot off.

I started to chase after him in a sort of half-walk, half-jog effort to catch up with him. Although I had lost weight, I still wasn't physically fit. I must have run nearly halfway round the pond by the time his hand grabbed my wrist and he pulled me down onto the picnic blanket.

Then I felt his lips touch mine. At first I pushed him away, as I felt it wasn't the time or the place, but mostly because it wasn't giving me a chance to take command of the situation. But then I let my heart rule my head and allowed my mind and body to go with the moment.

His left hand was holding my right cheek and the other was stroking my back. We kissed hard and passionately, his hands tweaking my hair at first and then venturing down towards my breasts. I had never felt so wanted. He put his hand under my top and caressed them, gently rubbing my nipples. Then I felt his penis pressing up against my thigh. I wasn't sure what to do, it was all too soon.

Should I let it go or wait? Heart or head?

Eventually, I let my head win. He was riding on top of me, grinding and rubbing his manhood against me. I must admit I was aroused, but I knew I couldn't go all the way with him. Not just yet. He grabbed my hand and moved it towards his penis, but I redirected it towards his bum and gave it a cheeky squeeze.

We were still kissing when he whispered in my ear, 'I want you, Bella. Oh my God, I've never wanted anyone more. I've got some condoms in the picnic bag.'

As he said that, I stopped kissing him and sat up, pushing him off me as I did so.

'Wooaahh! Just wait a minute! When and how did I give you the signal that "picnic" was code for "easy shag"?'

'I just thought that we got on so well. I thought it would be just what you needed,' he said, trying to grab my hand.

'Just what I needed? Just a few months after my life was turned upside down by a man, I need another man taking advantage of a situation and thinking it's just a shag I need to make it all OK? Well, newsflash! I'm not that kind of girl!'

I got up, shoved his hand away and marched back towards the site.

'Oh, Bella, come on. Please come back and have some food. Forget that it happened. Please, come on, let's start again. My blokedar's just completely off. Bella?!'

He ran after me and looked me straight in my eye. 'I'm sorry, Bella. I misread the signals. Please forgive me.'

The puppy dog eyes came out and I could do nothing other than smile. I had actually enjoyed the snogging and feeling wanted, and I had also secretly loved hearing him beg.

'OK, OK, let's have lunch. But no heavy petting. A pash here and there is more than welcome, though.' I gave him a kiss on the cheek to reinforce my words.

'Cool m'lady, let's do lunch.'

We made our way back to picnic blanket, which had to be straightened out before we could sit on it again.

The rest of the afternoon was idyllic. The sun shone, the company was ideal and Lou was the perfect gentleman. We did share the odd romantic moment, but we constrained ourselves to a long, lingering kiss here and there. I really wanted to shag his brains out, but I didn't want to be known as the site bike, and neither did I want to feel as though he was doing it out of pity. I had already felt like that for the last couple of years.

We made our way back to Sunnyside as the sun was going down and it was starting to get a little chilly. Lou put his arm around me and we walked in sync without saying a word.

'Do you want me to come in for a bit?' Lou asked with a wink, but it wasn't a sleazy wink.

'No, I'm bushed to be honest. I'd like to hit the sack and wake up a happy lady tomorrow. Thanks so much for an amazing day. I really enjoyed it.'

'No problem, Bella. You're great company, even if you don't put out,' he giggled.

'Eh, cheeky! Bog off to bed!' I turned around to get in my van with the hugest smile on my face. It was the best day I could remember in a very long time.

Chapter 11: The passion wagon

I slept like a log after all the fresh air, but I was awoken by an alarm call of twittering blackbirds singing to one another. I had managed to get some new material, in the old shed I found in a John Lewis bag with some lovely fabric folded ready to make a blind for the roof window, so at least I wasn't waking up because of the full glare of the sun, which was rising at silly o'clock now that it was summertime.

I needed to get up, showered and dressed early, as I had a busy day ahead of me. Fran had given me a long list of jobs and the keys of all the clients who were coming to visit their vans at the weekend. I had a lot of cleaning and gardening to crack on with over the following few days, which provided a nice distraction, because I didn't want to get too engrossed in the Lou-Fran-Bella love triangle. I had forgotten to ask him about the whole Fran thing, but I suppose part of me wanted to pretend it wasn't an issue.

After a few months of working at the site, it really felt like I was at home there. I enjoyed my job as there was no pressure and it was enjoyable. Half the time I was outside gardening in the sunshine, while the other half I was indoors cleaning the caravans to dodge the rain. I always had music with me.

I sometimes thought about Tim and wondered how he could have just walked away without even a thought of how I was or even if I had got home safely. I wondered whether his job was working out and whether he was living with 'the other woman'.

But my little grope with Lou had given me some much-needed self-confidence. I finally felt as though I was a worthy woman, who deserved to be loved for who I was. I had come to the conclusion that Tim was just really shallow. He could only see a woman in a fat suit; he couldn't see the warm, caring woman who would have done anything for him. For that reason, I realised he was no longer worthy of my thoughts. I obviously wasn't in his.

It started raining just as I headed out, so I decided that cleaning the caravans would be the best place to start. I set up the mp3 Fran had kindly bought me and got down to some scrubbing. One of my favourite summer tunes came on: 'Summertime' by Jazzy Jeff and The Fresh Prince.

'Summer, summer, summertime. Oooooo, summertime!' I sang at the top of my voice.

Just at that moment, Lou popped his head through the door. He looked a little damp from the drizzle, but he was still so hot!

'Hey! Was just checking a cat wasn't getting strangled in here.'

'Oi!' I said, chucking the wet cloth in my hand at him. It hit him straight in the face. *Result!*

'I love this song. Come on in out of the rain and make me a cuppa,' I said, pointing towards the kettle and my Tupperware box full of teabags and milk sachets.

'Wish I'd never popped in now. You just use and abuse me.'

'Ha! You wish!' In truth, I could think of all sorts of ways to abuse him!

Lou came in and made me a cuppa with my clear instructions that it was to be strong with no sugar.

I decided to ask him about Fran.

'So, have you known Fran long?' I asked in the most casual way possible.

'Yeah, years to be honest. We've always had the van here, so I've spent nearly every summer here with my parents since I can remember. We've spent so many good times with Fran and Justin.'

His eyes glazed over and I could tell he was reminiscing.

I had forgotten all about Justin.

'Oh right, so are you quite close to Fran?' I probed. I continued cleaning as I was still trying to maintain a casual air.

'We were, but so much now. Not since, well… Justin…' He shrugged.

Things were starting to get interesting.

'Since Justin what? I thought he was abroad?' I asked quietly.

'He is. Well he was kind of sent away. It's a long story.' He carried on making the tea.

'Oh right. Well, we have time…'

Go on, tell me! I thought.

'The short version is that Justin got a local girl pregnant, paid her to get an abortion and then took off after Fran paid for an around-the-world ticket because the villagers found out and started saying all sorts. The girl was telling everyone he had made her get an abortion or he would leave her, but to be honest they weren't really together. It was just a casual liaison, but anyway, Fran had a weird turn and the site went downhill for a few months. Fran doesn't like being ostracised by anyone, never mind being talked about by the whole village.'

Lou passed me the weakest cup of tea I had ever seen. He obviously hadn't stuck to the brief.

'Oh, that makes sense. I went into the village when I first got here and I heard some quite sarky comments from a couple of the locals when I mentioned I was working here.'

'It's all sorted now, though. As it happened, the girl got pregnant by another guy three months later, but sadly lost it, think it was stress related to 'gossiping' nosey villagers but everything calmed down.'

'So you're back here with Fran, then?' I might as well have asked him straight out if he was sleeping with her.

'Am I *back here with Fran?* That's an odd way of putting it. Yeah, we're all friends again. I even crashed on her sofa the other night after too many joints and a few too many glasses of wine. She's always good for some "peace out" company!' He winked at me again.

What did 'peace out' company mean? I wondered. *Did they or didn't they? I was more confused having asked the question than I had been before. Wasn't 'spending the night on the sofa' code for something? This was exactly why I didn't like relationships. As soon as people gave away a small part of themselves, their minds turned them into crazy, paranoid psychopaths who constantly need answers!*

I tried to change the subject. 'Any plans for tonight, or are you having another "peace out night" with Fran?' I couldn't have been more obvious if I had tried!

'Wooaah! Wait a minute… You think I…' He started laughing a little too hard for my liking. 'You think me and Fran have… Oh my God, dude! She's my mum's friend; my best mate's mum! I mean, you think I shagged Fran?!'

He stopped laughing and said, 'No, I haven't slept with and will never sleep with Fran. She's just a good listener and always has been. Ew, dude. Come on!'

He came over, put his arms around my waist and started kissing my neck. Then he turned me around, cupped my face in his hands and started kissing me with his soft, perfect lips. I couldn't help it. I dropped the cloths I had been holding and kissed him back, wrapping my arms around him.

We started pulling at each other's clothes and then Lou stopped. 'I haven't got... anything,' he said, breathless. He didn't need to explain what he meant.

I grabbed his hand and we ran over to my camper together through the willow. I couldn't remember where I had got the condoms from or why, but I was so pleased I had.

Before we knew it, Lou was inside me. He pushed me up on the sideboard, thrusting like he had the first time, only this time it was much more satisfying. I wrapped my legs around his waist and enjoyed every minute.

He laid me down on the bed and kissed my neck as he continued to thrust in and out. He started sucking my nipples and I could feel an orgasm coming. I grabbed his head and pulled him in for a kiss, then moments later I felt him quiver and he let out a gratified moan.

Then he rolled off and gave me a huge smile. 'Was it good for you?' he asked.

I just smiled back. He knew it had been good for me.

It was then that I heard Fran shouting for me.

'Oh shit, she'll be wondering where I am. I left the van open!' I started to dress as quickly as I could.

'Don't worry. Just tell her you nipped to the toilet, she'll be cool.'

Lou was completely relaxed and of course he was right. She wasn't to know what I had been doing. A broad grin spread across my face.

When I got back to the McKenzies' van I saw Fran and she looked stern. 'Where have you been? You left this van wide open.'

'Sorry, Fran, I just nipped to the loo.' This made me giggle as 'loo' and 'Lou' sounded exactly the same.

'But the toilet block's that way,' she said, looking puzzled.

'Erm, yeah, but it's ladies' time so I had to nip back to my camper.' I was impressed at how quickly I had thought of that.

'Oh, OK, well next time if you leave a van, make sure it's locked up. You just never know who's about.'

She turned on her heel and walked off.

She was acting a little out of character. I couldn't understand why she was being so funny. Had she seen me with Lou and realised what I had nipped back to the van for?

I decided I had better crack on and stop thinking. I had a lot to do before the weekend.

Chapter 12: Shower euphoria

The rest of the day flew by. It rained all day, but it was warm so it wasn't too bad. I couldn't stop thinking about Lou. I went from van to van in a haze of sexual pleasure, if there is such a thing. I hadn't been taken with such passion for so long that I had forgotten what passionate sex was all about.

By the time I had finished, it was nearly seven o'clock. The sun was just starting to melt down, but it was still light outside and had stopped raining at last.

I took myself off for a long shower. I needed it after the day's sweaty encounters, and cleaning was a real workout. I had received some good training in scrubbing while I was in the navy. The vans I had just cleaned were certainly shipshape.

I treated myself to a body scrub and shaved everywhere. Bikini weather was upon us and I didn't want my unkempt lady garden putting anyone off.

I was totally absorbed in my steaming shower when I heard, 'Hey! Room for one more?'

I automatically wrapped my arms around myself and then realised it was Lou.

'Oh my God! How did you get in here? The door was locked!' I said, pretending to tell him off.

He grabbed me closer and I could feel that he was already hard.

'You should check the door next time.' He nuzzled my neck and took me again.

I was in heaven, firstly because I had never had sex in the shower before, and secondly because I hadn't done it in the shower with a hot, ripped man before. I felt like I was in a movie. I rested my hands on the shower wall and let Lou make all the right moves.

He turned me around and lifted me up, and before I knew it I had come again and again. That was another first as I had never had a multiple organism before. I had read about them in a smutty book on a beach somewhere, but this was actually happening. To me!

Lou then bent me over and pounded me until he let out a roar of satisfaction. I was worried the whole site would have heard him, but I was determined to stay in the moment.

He gave me a kiss on the cheek, got dressed and disappeared as quickly as he had appeared. The shower was still red hot and steaming. I felt a bit dazed about what had just happened, but I welcomed it. It had made me feel euphoric.

Chapter 13: Lunch with the folks

Somehow, three weeks had passed since our encounter in the shower. I was working long hours, six days a week, so I had hardly seen Lou. He was still about, but I hadn't spent time with him as we had done before. However, the site was nearly up to scratch. The vans were all occupied and I was just doing general maintenance around the site and cleaning now.

My parents had announced that they would be paying me a visit. It was out of the blue, as although I was in fairly regular contact, I was so used to only seeing my folks a few times each year it hadn't occurred to me that they only lived an hour and a half away and could visit without too many road rage attacks on the way.

I was looking forward to seeing them, but I wasn't looking forward to the questions they would ask and all the explaining I would have to do. I had decided to keep it simple. I would tell them about the job, show them where I lived and that was that; nothing about Lou. To be honest, I wasn't sure about Lou myself. We were more or less friends with benefits, so I decided to keep that title to myself.

Fran had given me a long weekend off, as I had been grafting nonstop for a couple of weeks. I was looking forward to some chill time. The weather forecast was looking good, so I took myself down to the village to get some supplies for their visit and some flowers. Flowers always made the van look homely.

I didn't get into Bradbury much, but it always made me smile when I did. It was a lovely time of year with blossom on the trees. Magnolia trees, in particular, seemed very popular in the area. It was the kind of village where I wanted to stop and talk to everyone, but I always found everyone was talking to other people. Not once, apart from during my first visit, had anyone ever really tried to interact with me in a meaningful way.

But truth be told, I wasn't that bothered, as it seemed when I did talk to anyone in the village they were determined to taint my view of Fran. I guess it was based on snobbery about the caravan site. However nice Sunnyside was, it was located on the cusp of their chocolate box village.

I got back to the site and had an hour to spare before my parents arrived. I decided to have a quick shower and change.

All refreshed from my shower, I put on a baggy summer dress and plaited my hair. I was ready.

I kept looking at the clock in the van, as they should have arrived by this point. It was almost lunchtime. I was getting a little concerned, but then I heard my dad's booming voice coming from the site office. He was bellowing at my mum, as usual.

I was so excited about seeing them. It felt like it had been ages, and I suppose it had been about six months, which actually was ages.

I ran towards the site office to find them, and there they were, all confused and cute, as if they had just been spewed out into an episode of *The Good Life*.

'Mum! Dad!' I shouted, waving at them.

'Oh, Annabel! How are you?' Mum opened her arms and I ran into the cuddle as if I was four years old.

'Much better for seeing you guys. Where have you been? I was expecting you before now! I was getting worried.'

'Well, your mum said you lived in Bradford and the postcodes didn't match with a Bradford address, so we had to find where I had written your address down. Then your mother needed the loo, so we ended up wasting a lot of time faffing around. Anyway, how are you, chutney?' My dad gave me a one-armed cuddle. He was a tall man and I always felt safe in his embrace.

'Oh well, at least you're here now. I'm so pleased to see you! Come on, follow me. I'll show you my new pad.' I beamed with excitement, as this was the first time in months I had been in the company of people I actually knew.

'Come in, sit down,' I said when we reached my van, pointing towards the seats in the awning. It was a lovely warm day, so it almost felt like we were on holiday.

'So, Annabel, have you got some sort of Romany Gypsy in your blood?' My mum looked a little confused.

'I told you I lived on a caravan site. What exactly did you think I lived in?' My bubble of excitement was gradually deflating.

'What your mother means is, you seem to be attracted to these kinds of places,' my dad said, looking around.

'But this place has given me a job and a roof over my head after getting left here with nothing when Tim did one. What's wrong with it, anyway?' I could feel myself going on the defensive.

'Nothing, nothing at all. We just thought... well, nothing. It's lovely, and I love the willow opening. It's like a fairy tale.' Mum could see that I was getting anxious.

'It is, Mum, and it'll do till I get my head together and sort out what I want for the future.'

'You could always come home, you know, or even just visit at weekends or on your days off.' My dad was clearly worried.

'Look, I know this looks unconventional and a little unorthodox, but I've never felt happier than I have been the last few months. I've made some good friends and I feel really refreshed.' I had never spoken from the heart to my folks before, and it felt like a release to finally do so.

'Annabel, it obviously agrees with you. You've lost a few pounds, haven't you? All Dad and I want is for you to know that we're here for you, come rain or shine, and if that means picking you up in the middle of the night, then so be it. As long as you know we just want you to be happy.'

Mum had grabbed hold of my cheeks as if she was talking directly into my soul. At least, that's how it felt with her intense stare and her big boggly eyes looking straight at me from six inches away.

'Yes, chutney, that's all we want. Anyway, I'm starving. What do we do for dinner around here?' Dad had always been great at changing the subject, especially when he was hungry.

'Shall we go to the pub? There's a nice one just down from the canal.' I started to reminisce about Lou. I had missed him over the last few weeks. When the folks left, I fancied a bit of Lou time.

'Yes, chutney, sounds fine. How far is it? 'Cause you know with my dodgy knees and back I can't walk far.'

'It's not far, Dad, it's about a ten-minute walk away.' It was more like thirty, but he desperately needed the exercise. I decided I would have to talk to him about computers and ponds to distract him so that he didn't realise.

We seemed to get to the pub in no time at all, and I actually enjoyed our chat about motherboards and extra memory thingamajigs.

Mum trotted along behind us talking to the birds, bees and passers-by.

We had to sit inside as Mum has a thing about sitting outside because of the flies. I was a bit gutted, as it was the perfect day for dinner in the sun.

We ordered, which was always a nightmare with Mum. She always asked a hundred questions: What does it come with? Could she change the chips to a jacket? Could she have hot water with her pot of tea? How long will it take? Do you take credit cards? And so on and so forth.

It made me smile, though, as it was always the same process, no matter where we went. The waiting staff always had the same 'Really? Why so many questions?' expressions on their faces when my mum was talking to them.

Dad and I usually choose the same thing. I opted for fish and chips, as I had seen some come out and they looked gorgeous. Dad followed suit.

We started to make small talk about the family, and who was doing what. Most of my relatives lived in the Lincoln area, but some had moved further afield. I was an only child, which, on reflection, had always been great. I had always had my folks' full attention and support, and they had never seemed to feel the same pressure the parents of multiple kids I went to school with did. Their parents had always seemed so stressed and rushed. I had missed having a sister or brother to laugh and fight with, though.

My gaze had wandered through the window and into the beer garden. I could see two people looking into one another's eyes very intensely. They were deep in conversation. To my angst, I realised it was Fran and Lou!

What were they doing there, and why were they sitting so close?

I couldn't take my eyes off them.

'What's got your attention, chutney?'

'Erm, nothing. Just thought I'd seen someone I knew.'

When I looked out again they had gone.

But where? Were they on their way to her van for an afternoon of pleasure, Lou-style? I wondered.

I hoped not, as that was what I wanted for dessert. My eyes started to narrow as I mulled it over.

'Here's your fish and chips. Do you want any sauces?'

The waiter put a huge plate of food down in front of me.

'Erm, no thanks. Oh yes, sorry. Vinegar please.'

'Are you OK, Annabel? You seem really distant.'

'Sorry, Mum. Just hungry.'

I consciously turned my attention back to my folks.

'So, I was thinking, now we're practically neighbours we can see each other more often. Maybe I can come home the next weekend I get off. I haven't been back in ages. It would be nice to catch up with everyone.'

'That sounds wonderful. When's your next weekend off?'

Mum was clearly excited.

'I'm not sure. This is the first full weekend I've had off in ages. But if things are up to scratch and Fran's happy, I can't see that getting a weekend off here and there would be a problem.'

I smiled at Mum. Dad was too busy getting stuck into his fish to pay attention.

After dinner, we took a slower walk back to the site and Dad noticed the distance this time, and he complained most of the way..

'I'm sure it wasn't as far as this on the way here. My knees aren't what they used to be, you know.'

I was smiling inside, as I could have scripted him.

As I put the kettle on for a brew, I noticed a note attached to the window. It read:

Hey you, long time no see.
Let's hook up tonight,
Maybe in the shower...
Lou xxx

Really? Has he got that much cheek? I thought.

I couldn't believe he had spent the afternoon with Fran and thought he could just pick up where we had left off in the evening.

Men! All the bloody same!

'How's that brew coming? We'll need to make tracks soon, chutney, before it starts getting busy on the roads.' Dad was looking at his watch. He had a thing about 'rush hour', as if it was a new thing he had discovered, even though Sunday's are quiet Dad still had a thing bout 'rush hour' traffic!

'It's nearly done, Dad. Two minutes.' I was actually brewing up what I was going to say to Lou.

The two-timing scumbag!

Mum came in and took the drinks outside. 'This is lovely, Annabel. I can understand you being content here. I feel happier now that I've seen where you live and work.'

She pulled out an envelope and gave it to me. 'Here's some money to help with whatever. It seems the fresh air is shrinking you, so go and get some clothes that actually fit!' She gave me a lovely twinkly smile.

'Woooahh!' thanks Mum… and Dad. Shopping!'

Apart from the shorts I had bought, I couldn't remember the last time I had been clothes shopping.

'You're welcome, chutney, but you must come home soon for a visit. And we'll come back here soon. It's lovely, and like your mum said, you look well. And Tim… well, you're best rid of him.'

That was the first and last time Dad ever mentioned Tim after the breakup.

Chapter 14: Mixed emotions

I felt a bit deflated after they had left, and even shed a few tears. I wondered whether I should have gone with them. I'm not usually one to feel sorry for myself or wrapped up in my own drama, but it felt like the only people in the world who truly loved me had just left me and I was all alone. Loneliness is such an isolating thing. It can make you feel alone even in a crowded room.

Just at that moment, Lou popped his head around the door.

Damn that man! He always knows the perfect time to turn up! I thought.

'Hey, have you been crying?' He lifted my chin up and looked into my eyes. 'Aw, Bell, what's up?' He gave me a cuddle and I sank into his chest, sobbing like a baby.

'What's been happening? Why are you so upset?'

'Oh, it's just life, that's all. My parents were here today and I guess I miss them.' I was still cuddled up to him.

'You didn't mention your parents coming, you should have said. I met up with Fran for lunch, but I would have come and met them if I'd known.'

And there it was. He had told me without being asked.

But had it just been lunch, or had he seen me with my folks and felt the need to explain? Aargh, he was either really good at covering his tracks or he was telling the truth.

'Oh, did you? Was it nice?'

I should have just said, 'Yeah, I saw you', but I didn't.

'Yeah, it was OK. She told me Justin's on his way back from the Far East. She said he'll be back by next weekend as he's stopping off in Dubai or somewhere first.'

'How come just you and Fran went? Why didn't your parents go with you?'

'Well, to be honest, my parents don't really like Justin. He tried it on with my mom before he left, just after he got Katy pregnant, so he's not everyone's favourite person. She wanted to tell me 'cause she was concerned about him coming back. He's not been gone as long as he was supposed to be and Fran's already had to convince him twice not to come back so early, but it seems this time he's determined to return. Fran wants me to tell my mum, but to be honest she was quite flattered by his attentions. It was my dad who was really miffed, as me and Justin have known each other since we were kids.'

Lou was pacing around the awning, letting off verbal steam. It seemed I wasn't the only who needed to have a blowout.

'So how come, when I first met you, all of you were round Fran's like a long-lost family?'

'Well we are, I suppose. It's just that when Justin's not there we don't mention him. As soon as he's around it's like a dysfunctional family.

'Hell yeah! Sounds like Oprah needs to get involved!' I flashed him a massive smile and gave his hand a cheeky tug. He looked like a lost little boy.

'I just miss how it used to be. Me and Justin were like bros. I know we didn't see each till summertime, but we spent every day together here, doing... well, what boys do.'

'Do you mean smoking weed?' I looked at him quizzically.

'Erm, maybe! How did you guess?' He smirked.

'I was high from the fumes for the first couple weeks living in the van! And it's not as if Fran's against it. She's a right dope head!' I started laughing. 'It seems everyone's keeping secrets that don't need keeping. So, in effect, the secrets are getting bigger and turning into lies,' I said.

'Yeah, you're so right. I think I should try and straighten everything out when Justin gets home.' And with that he swanned off.

Oh, OK, great. Me and my big mouth, and my 'peace out, man' ideas!

'But I think someone needs me first,' Lou said, suddenly reappearing through the canvas.

'I thought you'd forgotten me!'

He stroked my hair. 'How could I forget you, my little Bell? You seem to be the only thought in my head at the moment.'

He started to kiss me in a gentle and loving way. It felt totally different from the way he had kissed me before. It had always seemed urgent and full of passion previously, but this was just a gentle, loving kiss, as if we were in a relationship.

I loved the way he made me feel. His accent made me laugh because he often came out with American sayings in a Wigan accent. I liked his big, soft hands and his strong, muscular body, which wrapped around me when we embraced. But most of all, he made me love myself, and somehow he even made me like myself again.

After we had made love, we fell asleep and slept through until the morning. Lou loved cuddling, and I always felt wrapped up in him like a blanket. I wasn't sure if it was because it was a tad small in the van or because he was a natural hugger, but either way it was nice.

'Do you fancy breakfast and some proper coffee somewhere? There's a good place in Lune.'

'Morning. You're awake then?'

Well, obviously, seeing as he was asking me a question.

'Yeah, baby. Can't you feel me?' He was stabbing me with his morning glory.

'Yes! Morning, Mr Willy.' I gave him a stroke, and one thing led to another. Before I knew it, we were entangled and Lou was back to being the lustful man from before. He had his hands on my breasts and was pounding me from the side, slowly at first and then faster, holding the back of my neck.

Then he flipped me around so I was on top. He grabbed my breasts again and raised himself up so he could slide my nipples into his mouth. He moved from one to the other as though he didn't want to leave one out. I leaned back and tickled his balls, which made him wince with pleasure. I could feel myself coming and let out a quiet shriek, and at the same time Lou came and grabbed my arms tightly.

Afterwards, we gave each other a satisfied glance and I collapsed onto the bed.

'Oh, how I love my days off!'

'And how I love you having days off!'

'Right, let's get showered and grab some breakfast.'

Lou jumped out of bed with the condom still attached. It was so unattractive! It looked like some sort of weird attachment, but he soon pulled it off and walked over to the shower block with just a towel around his waist.

After he had gone, I just sat there thinking, *Surely this isn't my life! Have I just fallen into a novel? Because six months ago I was sat in a freezing cold, rotting caravan eating crisps and watching Oprah!*

Chapter 15: A change of plans

I lay there waiting for Lou to finish in the shower, listening to the birds. Every now and again I heard a shriek from a child in a nearby caravan. Only a few of them had small children, but they were good kids in my estimation. They were polite, pleasant and liked having fun.

Most nights they were in their caravans, either asleep or watching telly by nine, but they got up quite early. This usually wasn't a problem as I was up before them for work. I could hear the McKenzies' boys singing 'Don't stop moving' by S club 7, but I found myself humming along to it.

'Right, your turn.' Lou had returned and caught me by surprise by chucking his wet towel over my face.

'Aw, thanks a lot!' I was not impressed with his laddish behaviour.

'Right, I'll nip into the shower and then do you fancy a trip to Nottingham? My folks gave me some pennies to get some new clothes" I spread the money out like a fan.

'Wahooo! We can we get some lunch out of that, too.' He winked at me.

'NO!' I called out as I went to take a shower.

I still loved going for my daily shower, as I kept it in pristine condition. Not many people used it, but whoever else did also looked after the facilities carefully.

I was so looking forward to getting some new clothes. It would be interesting to see what size I needed. I knew I had lost weight, but I wasn't sure to what degree. My size sixteens definitely didn't fit, and my size fourteens were very loose.

I felt I needed to change the way I approached shopping. I had always bought baggy sacks to hide every inch of my body; even the jeans I bought were shapeless and baggy. I never wore leggings as I didn't like the shape or size of my legs.

But since I had become more active and been on the go for up to ten hours a day, my body had changed a lot. I was actually starting to get sort of toned.

I would definitely need new undies and I needed to get my boobs measured properly. I wasn't sure I needed a 38GG bra any more as my boobs were beginning to look like golf balls in the nineteenth hole. I also wasn't sure my comfy granny pants were that attractive now that I was having sex again.

When I got back to the van, Fran was there.

'Hi Fran, everything OK?'

'Yes, darling, everything's fine. Look, I'm sorry to do this, but I need you to work today. I've just had a call from Justin. He's in Dubai, but he'll be landing this afternoon and I said I would pick him up. So I really need you to stay here and hold the reins for me until I get back. I have to pick him up from

London and I'm planning on staying over.' She was pulling a strange, childlike, pleading face.

Oh, for God's sake! Why today of all fucking days? I thought. *The day I want to go shopping for the first time in years with actual money, and not just to drool through a shop window.*

But Fran had helped me in so many ways and had given me a second chance at life. It was the least I could do.

'Aw, that's lovely, Fran. Bet you can't wait to see him. He's been away for a while, hasn't he?' I asked through gritted teeth, trying my hardest to sound genuine.

'Great stuff, thanks so much. Oh, and you can come out from under the bed now, Lou!' She winked at me and then pointed at him, whispering, 'He's a keeper' in my ear as she left.

Really? How does she know that? I wondered.

The old questions were swirling around in my head again.

Why had Lou hidden under the bed? Had it really mattered that Fran had seen him there?

I still wasn't really sure about all that 'she's like a mom to me' bullshit.

Argghhhh! I felt so pissed off, but I needed to keep my thoughts to myself and try to chill out. I shoved on one of my oversized dresses and wrapped a belt around my waist, tying it so tight I nearly burst my intestines.

'Hi Belllllaaaa! Are we OK?' Lou asked.

'No, not really. I'm a bit pissed off. I mean, look at me. I've got a dress on that looks like shite and I have nothing else that fits. It's just rubbish. I was really looking forward to looking good and feeling great.'

I flopped onto the bed and cried. It was a bit overdramatic, but it was the natural overflow of all my pent-up emotions.

'Hey, come on, gorgeous. You don't need fancy dresses to be you. You are who you are, and that's Bella. Beautiful, funny, sexy, intelligent Bella.'

Lou wrapped his arms around me and scooped me up into a massive cuddle, which was exactly what I needed.

'I know, but I was so looking forward to going shopping. It's not about buying things; it's about putting aside the old me and saying hi to the new me. And now I'm just like a bad penny that came back.' I sobbed onto Lou's arm, leaving a trail of snot.

'Look at me. Is that what this is all about? Tim and your old life? You don't need new clothes to be rid of that. You're already rid of that! It was over the day that nob left you with nothing apart from the clothes in your suitcase. So really those clothes are the new you anyway, as you were left here together.'

Lou was trying his best to philosophise, but all it did was make me giggle.

I had never heard so much crap in all my life!

'Yeah, you're right. Onwards and upwards, eh? Well I'm not really working today. Shall we go to Bradbury and get some wine? We can sit on Fran's decking and sunbathe all afternoon.' I wiped away my tears, which had become tears of laughter by this point.

'Hell yeah, baby. I'll give Ma and Pa a shout later on if you like and get Mom to light the barbecue up.' He looked convinced that he had made a massive accomplishment in counselling me.

'Sounds perfect,' I said, and it did.

Who needs new clothes anyway? I thought. *Well, me, but they can wait.*

Chapter 16: Thinking ahead

I headed back early after the barbecue. I wanted to be up bright and early to start back at work, especially as Fran would be coming back with the prodigal son.

I was quite intrigued about meeting him. I had seen photos of Justin, but they were all pictures with him in the distance or in a group of lads with his head in a headlock or a scrum rather than in full view. From what I had seen of him, though, he definitely looked handsome in a 'cool dude' kind of way.

I had asked Lou to stay with his folks, which he hadn't been too happy about. He had looked like a deflated balloon when I told him I was heading back without him. I needed some space and rest. It had been a busy couple of days, what with my parents' visit and the failed shopping day.

I woke up as normal the next day to the sound of twittering blackbirds and trilling robins. They always reminded me of the ducks. Deep down, I had loved those ducks.

I contemplated my next plan of action.

Should I go for tea or coffee?

I had gone off coffee just lately, but there was nothing like a morning brew to get the body oiled up and ready to go. I flicked the kettle on and decided to have a good old cuppa.

I relaxed for a while. Looking around the van, it was lovely and cosy. It was particularly quaint in this weather. It was so nice and warm most days and pleasant at night. The wind chimes whispered tales of the willow trees, and the decor was so retro and happy. It made me feel relaxed and calm. I had started to contemplate my future, despite the idyllic situation I was living in. I didn't relish the idea of spending another winter in a campervan, however cute it was.

I knew I would need to start looking for a more permanent solution. I had a few more months before the autumn nights started turning cold and dark.

I wasn't sure what I could do. I wasn't qualified to do anything apart from looking at a radar screen or firing an AK47, and there wasn't much call for that in everyday life. I could become a bodyguard for the royal family or guard Buckingham Palace like 007, but I also had a licence to make a mean brew!

I wondered if I should start putting together a CV, but I wasn't sure who would want to employ me. I had joined the navy at nineteen, left at twenty-two, been jobless for nearly two years and then become a caravan caretaker.

I suppose the new role hadn't pigeonholed me, and it showed I could adapt to new challenges and was willing to take on adverse roles. I decided I had better write that down before I forgot it.

After my brew and a bit more soul-searching, I turned my thoughts back to real life and what the day ahead would bring. I knew the grass had to be cut across the whole site and that would take most of the day.

I'd better crack on before the boss arrives, I thought.

Chapter 17: Keeping it simple

It was a lovely day to cut the grass: cloudy with hints of sunshine, and nice and warm. I had half the park done by lunchtime. I didn't really want to stop, as I was hoping for an early finish, but I was starving and needed a break and some juice.

I had managed to have a good old natter with most of the residents who were in. Mrs Brown gave me a good rundown about her arthritis and about living in Scottish border territory. It hadn't done her arthritis any good, apparently, but the warmth of 'the south' always made her feel better. It made me laugh when Mrs Brown referred to Sunnyside as down south, but it obviously was to her.

Mrs Paulson loved telling me about her holidays: where she had been, where she was going and for how long. She always made me stop for tea and biscuits, which I never turned down. Old habits and all that.

Mr Benison was a little odd as he mostly came by himself. He loved to go fishing in the fishery up past the canal. His wife came every now and again, but she was very quiet and was rarely seen out and about.

Most of the residents had a good old story to tell, even if that meant they told me the same things over and over again. I figured that once folk got past sixty-five they didn't care what they said or to whom; they just liked a natter.

I had a very quick chat with Jude. She was as flamboyant as ever, overdramatising the drive down as always. She was also surprised at the way Lou had left the caravan in pristine condition as if he hadn't been there. The thought crossed my mind that he had been with me, but some days I hadn't seen him at all, so that didn't explain it entirely.

Jude was whittling away about what Lou was going to do with his philosophy degree. It blew me away as she talked about it; it made sense of the way he had been talking to me the other day.

He actually had been trying to philosophise, bless him. He must have seen me as a subject!

She said he had finished university in December after four years of study, apart from having to go back for the odd exam. He hadn't worked since, although he had helped with some of Lucas' business ventures in the States and in Wigan. She didn't elaborate on that much. It suddenly dawned on me that I hadn't really talked much to Lou about his life. How awful and selfish of me not to have taken any notice of the guy I had been shagging for the past couple of weeks.

'You talk to him, Annabel. Try and get some sense out of him and see where his future's going, darlin', cause he might just listen to you. He sure ain't listening to me or his pa.' She looked sad as she said this.

'Erm, I will if you want me to, but I can't say that I'll make much difference. We don't really talk about much.'

Jude looked at me with raised eyebrows. She didn't need to explain what she was thinking: *I bet you don't!*

I turned scarlet in response, as it made me sound so cheap!

After a quick break, I decided to keep on trucking as I didn't have much more to do and I wanted to chill with my book and a cuppa in the late afternoon sun. It always surprised me that, however warm it was outside, a cuppa was still the best source of refreshment.

I hadn't seen Lou and was wondering if he would pop by. I wondered what he did during the days and nights when he wasn't around. He seemed to disappear and then pop up a couple of days later. I wasn't sure if he went back to Wigan every now and then or was closer to home.

I should have asked Jude, but I didn't want to start making whatever was between us serious. If I started asking too many questions, it would sound as though I cared and was keeping tabs on him. I was a little confused about where he was disappearing to, though. But then I asked myself why I always had to overcomplicate a situation that really didn't need to be complicated.

Chapter 18: The prodigal returns

I finished at three, had a quick shower, opened a can of beer to celebrate the day's work and sat in the late afternoon sun. It was so pleasant. I dragged the table and chairs out of the awning and positioned them under the trees for a bit of shade, as I had been out in the sun all day.

I was so enjoying my book and my beer, I actually found myself saying out loud, 'This is the life!'

'Annabel, where are you?'

It was Fran's voice. She must have been looking for me in the van.

'Hi Fran, I'm over here. Under the birch.' I couldn't be bothered to move.

'Oh, there you are. Well, the site smells and looks divine. I love the smell of cut grass.'

'Did you pick up Justin?' I asked, looking at her over my sunglasses.

'Yes! Justin, come over here and meet Annabel!' She looked for him through the willow.

'I'm coming,' he replied in a strange, half-posh, half-country accent.

And there he was, the elusive Justin. He wasn't what I had been expecting at all. He was smaller than I had imagined, probably about five foot eight, and he had a slight beer belly. He looked like his mum, with a long face and pronounced cheekbones, but he had a very masculine, chiselled jawline, an amazing tan, and sun-streaked hair, which was short and wavy, but just long enough to run your fingers through. I couldn't quite make out his eye colour, but they looked hazel in the sunlight.

His dress sense was about as bad as mine. He wore cut-off, knee-length jeans with a Metallica vest top. I approved of his taste in music, though.

'Hello, Annabel. Mum hasn't stopped singing your praises. Do you mind if I join you for a beer?' And with that he pulled up a chair and sat himself down.

It was rather presumptuous. I had been quite happy chilling in my own company.

'Erm, yeah, take a seat. I'll get one for Fran too.' I turned to face Fran but she had gone. She had left me to babysit! I grabbed Justin a beer from the fridge.

'So, did you have a nice flight?' I asked, thinking it best to be sociable.

'Yeah, it was OK. I'm glad to be home, although I see you've taken the roof from over my head.' He looked over at me with raised eyebrows.

'Oh shit, I hadn't even thought about that. I suppose you'll need me to move out?' I was starting to panic a bit. It hadn't even registered with me that I was living in his pad.

Where would I go? There were no spare caravans on the site.

'Don't worry. Mum and I have already discussed it and I'm going to bunk in with her. I was only pulling your leg. She's got plenty of room, and compared to this place it's like a mansion.' Justin grinned at me and gave me a shoulder nudge.

'Oh right, brilliant. I was starting to panic a bit.' I think the expression on my face had already given this away.

We sat chatting for a while and then he suddenly stood up.

'My round. Another beer?' He was on his way to the fridge.

I shook my can and there was still a bit left in it. *Oh well, bottoms up!* I thought.

'Yes please, if you're going that way.'

For some reason, I felt quite relaxed with Justin. I wasn't sure if it was his familiarity or the fact that he was talkative like Fran. I felt at ease with him, as if I had known him since our school day.

'Oops, best nip to the shop for some more beer. Here, you have this one. I don't want to be caught drinking and driving on my first day back! I won't be long.' He threw the can at me and strolled off through the willow.

What a bizarre meeting, I thought.

I had felt very lumbered with him about an hour earlier, and now I was looking forward to his return. It was good to have someone of my age around. I loved the stories and chinwags I had with some of the older residents, but talking about music and having a beer with a fellow twenty-something was quite satisfying.

'Hello, there. It's only me. Annabel, Justin?'

'Over here, Fran!' I hadn't moved from where I had been sitting before, so I had no idea why she was announcing her presence so clearly. Unless she felt as though she might have been interrupting something.

'Oh, there you are. Where's Justin? Has he nipped to the loo?' She was looking around curiously.

'He's just nipped to the supermarket to get some more beers.'

'He's what?!' Why did you let him? Oh my... what if... oh no!' Fran was visibly distressed. She started pacing back and forth like a caged animal.

'Sorry, Fran, have I done something wrong? I wasn't aware that I was meant to keep him here.'

Fran was making me distressed. Then it dawned on me about the girl he had got pregnant, the rumours, the villagers and her sending him off to explore the world. It just hadn't occurred to me to keep him on site.

'Do you want me to go down to the village?'

I stood up and held Fran, who looked as though she was about to have a nervous breakdown.

'No, no, it'll be fine. Where's he going? The express? Who works there?' I could see she was making a mental note of who worked where and which days; contemplating anyone Justin could possibly bump in to.

'Fran, calm down...'

'I am calm, Annabel. If only you'd done your job properly!' She shouted at me with conviction. Then she sat down and cried.

Woaaah! I hadn't realised babysitting Fran's wayward son was in my remit. I knew she was upset but there was no need for that.

I had given up a weekend of shopping with Lou to look after the site for her. Thinking of Lou, he seemed to have done another disappearing act.

'Let's get this party started!' came a voice, and through the willow with boxes of beer came Lou and Justin. They looked like naughty schoolboys who had just got back from a field trip.

'Oh, thank God! Where have you been?'

'Hey, Fran, chill. Everything's fine. I always look after my bro!' Lou put an arm around Justin's shoulder and gave an excited fist pump with the other.

'Mum, what on earth's the matter? It looks like you've been crying.' Justin crouched down to get a better look at her.

'What do you think the matter is, Justin? I mean, really, what could it be?' She was starting to look relieved, despite her direct questions.

'Mum, I can't run away and never show my face around the village. Everyone's talking about someone else's life now, anyway. I'm a big boy and I'll handle it. I created the problem, so I'll fix it.' He gave his mum a hug.

I felt slightly awkward, as I hadn't been told any of the details by Fran. All the information I had came from Lou, but she must have assumed that I knew.

It was hard living in such a small village. Fran probably felt talked about and isolated, when the reality was that people quickly tended to move on to new gossip and to medalling in someone else's life.

Justin had done right in my book. He had gone into the village, bold as brass, as if nothing had ever happened. But whatever had happened was just hearsay anyway, and far worse things happened in towns and cities. It was only in places like Bradbury that everything got exaggerated and magnified.

What had started out as a story of 'boy meets girl, boy gets get pregnant and they decide to get an abortion' had turned into 'boy meets girl, boy gets girl pregnant and forces her to get an abortion, and then boy gets sent away before he is publicly flogged on the village green'.

'I know, I know. I just worry. Right then, barbecue at my van. Lou, ask your folks round and let's get this welcome home party going.' Fran jumped up and swished off through the willow trees.

I opened the warm beer I had been nursing since Justin had thrown it at me. I had been waiting for it to stop fizzing so that it didn't spew up all over my face.

'Best put these babies in the fridge,' said Lou as he disappeared into my van.

I was starting to feel like my home had become a communal dosshouse, where I just happened to sleep. Justin was carrying on as if he had never left, and Lou was just being Lou.

But I was glad he was there, putting his usual laidback twist on the situation.

Chapter 19: Wet and wild

Justin went through his music collection and put on a very eclectic mix, ranging from S club 7 to Nirvana. The boys pratted about, singing at the tops of their voices and dancing, or at least that's what they would have called it. I just sat and observed as I let them reminisce and find one another again. It was like watching a wildlife programme where baby chimpanzees were play-fighting and grooming each other at the same time.

'Another beer, Bellllllllaaaaa?' Lou shouted over to me.

'Yes please!' I got up and turned the music down a bit. The boys kept turning it up every time a good tune came on, but I didn't want to annoy Mrs Paulson as her van wasn't far from mine and they weren't soundproofed. Even though it was early, it would still be annoying for her.

'Hey, what's with the tunes?' Lou said, turning it back up.

'Lou, think about the neighbours!'

'Boring! Bella's boring!'

He grabbed me round the waist and slapped a massive kiss on my lips. Weirdly, I didn't embrace it. I felt a little embarrassed kissing him in front of Justin.

But Justin was sitting with his fifth can, looking chilled and not taking a blind bit of notice.

Lou was getting horny, I could tell by the movement in his trousers.

Jeez, time and a place and all that. Give a man a can and it turns him into a rampant rabbit!

'Lou, not here,' I whispered in his ear.

'Where then?' he whispered back into mine. 'Shower room?' He squeezed my bum softly and winked.

We both looked over at Justin, who had fallen asleep. The jet lag must have finally kicked in. I walked over to the shower block, which fortunately was unoccupied. Lou sprinted past me like a naughty schoolboy, whispering 'Beat you' as he overtook.

When I eventually got there, Lou had locked himself in the shower room, so I had to knock on the door. He opened it and grabbed me, drawing me close to him. We started pulling at each other's clothes as if there was a time limit on shagging each other's brains out.

He started slowly sucking my nipples, one at a time. He gave them a little nip with his lips and swished his tongue around them as if he was searching for them. Then he moved further down and parted my lips with his tongue. He licked my pussy and I started to feel a slow, rising pleasure. As he sucked and licked, he put his fingers tenderly up inside me. I was all of a quiver. I needed to sit down or hold on to something.

I raised up onto my tiptoes as I felt I was about to come, but before I could he stood up, sucked each nipple in turn and then lent me against the wall, which made me wince as my bare bottom touched the cold side. He crouched down a little and then entered me with force, but I was wet and felt engorged in pleasure.

He pushed in and out, holding my hands up above my head. Then he turned me around and I bent over as he pounded me. I could hear his balls smashing against my behind. He held the back of my neck as he got faster and faster, but he wasn't finished. He pulled out of me slowly and then sat in the shower and gestured for me to come over. He lowered me onto his penis and I slowly rode him as he sucked and softly bit my nipples.

Then he lent back a bit and I moved faster. I held onto his shoulders, as I could feel myself coming. As I did, Lou let out his coming groan.

'Don't stop, I'm coming,' he whispered.

I rode him faster and faster, until I screamed with pleasure. I had never done that before and it took me by surprise. I collapsed on top of him, with his penis still inside me. We panted and got our breath back. Then he kissed me and started stroking my hair.

'That was amazing, Bella. Shall we do it again?'

He held my face in his hands and I could feel him getting hard again.

Is he for real? I thought. *But I wasn't going to say no!*

Chapter 20: Grubs up!

When we finally got back to my van, Justin had disappeared. I guessed he was over at his mum's place. We grabbed some cans and had a wander over, hand in hand, but in silence.

I could smell the barbecue as we got closer, and as soon as I had people in my sights I dropped Lou's hand. I don't know why, but holding hands made it feel too serious for what I wanted at that moment.

'Hey, there you are!' Jude yelled over to us, beaming at Lou.

'Hi Mom. Sorry, have you been waiting for us?'

'Yes, we have, actually. Justin came over about an hour ago saying he had no idea where the pair of you were,' Fran said, looking a little miffed as she guarded the barbecue.

It smelt lush and I was starving.

'We went to get some more beers as Justin had fallen asleep.' Lou held the beers aloft in a bid to mask our deception.

I found a seat on the decking and chilled out. I wasn't really interested in chitchat, I was too hungry.

Justin came out of the van, and he and Lou did a weird hug-punch as they greeted one another. Lucas was tucked away in a corner, while Jude and Fran were deep in conversation. I was trying to hear what they were saying, but they were very good whisperers.

I sat alone for a while, feeling a tad invisible as everyone else was engaged in conversation, but I enjoyed watching the way Jude kept checking out Fran's boobs at every chance she got before sticking her own chest out, as if to compare. It was quite funny to watch, as Jude was so glam and always made-up. She looked more my age than I did, whereas Fran had a much more eccentric approach. She always wore purples and greens. She looked cool, though. I liked her effortless style.

The boys were still performing man gestures with one another. I guessed they had a lot of catching up to do. They hadn't had a proper conversation since Justin had got back. I wondered what Justin had got up to during his time away. If it was anything like what he had been up to while he was home I was sure he would have some good stories to tell.

Then there was Lucas, a nice, friendly old man. He was obviously loaded, but rather than buy an apartment in Spain or somewhere exotic, he had bought a static caravan in the Nottinghamshire countryside. It all seemed a bit odd, as if he had stuck a pin in a map and here they were. If I had lived in Wigan, I'm sure I would have wanted to be beside the sea rather than be landlocked at Sunnyside.

But I supposed it was their retreat. They had been coming here for years and in the summer they didn't often go home. Lucas went back every other week to catch up on work, I assumed. I wasn't sure what he did, but I guessed it was something to do with importing and exporting, judging by the fact that Lou regularly went to the States on his dad's behalf.

It was starting to get a bit cooler, so I wrapped a throw around my shoulders. I felt really at ease with the people around me. I had only known them a short while, but I felt as close to them as if they were family.

'Right, grubs up my darlings!' called Fran.

These were the words I had been waiting for, as I had started to consider eating my own head.

Chapter 21: Shop till I drop

I had the following day off, and I managed to sneak away from the barbecue early so I didn't feel hungover in the morning. The early drinks had done me in as I wasn't used to drinking as much by this point. I could drink the odd beer or glass of wine, but I was well out of practice in the art of lengthy drinking.

I decided to take the bus into Nottingham to get myself some clothes, as the lack of choice I had was becoming ridiculous and Mum's money was burning a hole in my pocket.

I knew there was a bus from Bradbury every hour, on the hour. If I got a wriggly on I could get the ten o'clock bus. It took an hour to get to Nottingham as the bus stopped at every village along the way.

I wasn't in any rush to get back, anyway. Lou hadn't come round the previous night. I guessed he had got caught up with the whole 'Justin returns' party and ended up crashing in Fran's van.

I got my stuff together and made my way to Bradbury. While I waited at the bus stop, I observed the comings and goings of the locals. It was a busy little place, considering there wasn't much there. A lady in her mid-forties sat next to me, chain-smoking cigarettes like they were going out of fashion. I assumed she was smoking so much because she wouldn't be able to have another one for an hour. It was bad to think she couldn't go an hour without a fag. I couldn't stand them, and it was starting to make me feel ill. Without realising it, I had moved about five metres away from the human chimney.

The bus was bang on time, which was lucky as I couldn't wait to get out of the 'fresh' air.

We snaked through the tiny villages, picking up little old ladies with their trolleys, mums with their prams, and men and women in business suits, who were obviously heading out for meetings or just starting work. It was a very eclectic mix of people, but they all had their papers or books ready for the journey.

I, on the other hand, stared out of the window and watched the world go by, making a mental note of the village names as we went along. I also started to make a list of the places I wanted to go: M&S for underwear and River Island for clothes. I loved the clothes in there, so I would be making a beeline for them.

Before I knew it, we were there at the bus station in Nottingham. I didn't know which way to go, so I decided to follow the crowd. They all seemed to know where they were going and even the little old ladies with trollies were going the same way.

It didn't take long to reach a shopping centre; it was straight across from the bus park. As I walked through the automatic doors, I felt my arms tingle with excitement. I had never really been into clothes, but this was like the new dawn of me.

Let's do this! Take me to the shops! I thought to myself.

To my amazement, one of the first shops I came across was River Island!

Wahoo! Come to me, clothes, I mused.

I walked around, swishing various items across my body in front of the mirror, checking out my reflection and trying to work out whether they would suit me. I was looking for casual clothes: jeans, a few fitted T-shirts and floaty dress tops, and some leggings and shorts.

But what size would I go for? Fourteen or twelve?

'Hi there, do you need any help?' a student-aged shop assistant asked me.

'Erm, no, thank you. Not at the moment.'

I felt embarrassed as I had a coat hanging round my neck and was swishing back and forth. I had positioned a dress underneath it that was fit only for a wedding, but I was transfixed by how feminine it was. I decided to take the plunge and try size twelve tops and size fourteen bottoms.

'Hi, how many have you got there? Looks like you're buying for everyone in here!' said a tall, slim, trendy dressing room assistant.

That pissed me off straight away. *To her, I was just a frump with no dress sense and very little knowledge of what was in fashion.*

Trendy girl showed me to a cubicle and helped me hang the garments up.

With a cheerier 'Shout if you need any help', she was off.

'Oh God, where do I start?' I said very loudly to myself without thinking.

As if I had a fairy godmother, trendy girl pulled the curtain back and, with a massive smile on her face, said, 'With these'.

She stretched out her arms, which were laden with clothes, and took away all the ones I had chosen, apart from a daisy-print see-through shirt.

'Hmmm, I think I'd like this on you,' she said, holding it out to me.

She put together several outfits, arranged them how they should be worn: either tucked in or out; with a belt or just ruffled.

'Right then, let's get started. If you need different sizes, give me...'

'...a shout!' I interjected with a smile.

With that, she strode off again.

I sat and looked at the outfits she had picked out. She had brought navy shorts and a white shirt; a yellow dress with a spring print and a white belt; and long, skinny jeans with a pale blue shirt and a big blue belt. I decided to start with the dress.

She had got me a size twelve, but it looked tiny on the hanger. I stripped off and looked at myself for the first time in months in a full-length mirror. I wasn't quite sure whether to be pleased or disgusted at the ripples that were still left, not to mention the stretch marks near my thighs.

Just what I wanted to see!

I unzipped the dress and pulled it over my head. I tried to tug it down over my boobs, but there was no chance, it was just pushing them south. There was no chance it was going over those puppies.

I pulled it back over my head, sat down and just looked straight ahead.

What was I thinking? A twelve, indeed!

'Hi, so how's it going?'

Trendy girl pulled the curtain open and I quickly pulled the yellow dress over me to cover myself up.

'Erm, well, I'm not a twelve. This wouldn't even get past my boobs.' I must have looked thoroughly defeated.

'Well that's probably because you need to unzip it and step into it.' She pointed to the zip.

'Oh right!' I blushed.

What a nob!

When she had left, I unzipped it, stepped in and zipped it back up. I could have cried.

It looked amazing!

After that, I was like a turbo model changer, trying on one outfit after the next. There were some little disappointments when I had to ask for a fourteen, but trendy lady assured me a size fourteen was really a twelve in other store's sizes. And besides, they looked good whatever the size, so I kept them in a 'to buy' pile. I sneaked back some of the clothes I had chosen, as I really liked the short dungarees and cargo pants in pink and khaki. I had to have some casual clothes to slob about in.

Trendy lady helped me transport all my purchases to the tills. They asked me if I wanted to open a store card, which would save me twenty percent on my first shop. It was tempting, as it would have saved me a lot of money.

I felt the devil on one shoulder saying, 'Do it! Buy now, pay later!' But the angel on the other shoulder was saying, 'You don't get owt for nowt!'

I went with the angel, as I had the money and wanted to avoid getting caught in a trap. I didn't need a stash of cash lying around, as I had very few outgoings.

'Right then, that'll be a grand total of £356.23. Will you be paying cash or by credit card?'

Trendy lady looked pleased with her handiwork.

'There you go,' I said, handing over the cash. 'And thanks so much for your help. You've steered me towards a new me.' I actually meant this, although it sounded rather corny.

'You're welcome. Come back again soon,' she said, passing me the bags.

I couldn't believe I had bought all that in one shop. I would have to head home as the plastic handles were already cutting into my hands. It felt like they were burning into my very bones. But I felt quite chuffed with myself. I had taken advice from a stranger and stepped out of my comfort zone. The new Bella Mac was in town!

Chapter 22: In with the new

I felt so exhausted by the time I got back that I couldn't even be bothered to empty out the bags. I was starting to wonder where I was going to put all my lovely new clothes as there wasn't much hanging space in the camper. There was only a makeshift hanger I had made out of some bungie cord, which hung across the side of the van. I would have to have a clear-out.

Out with the old and in with the new!

Not today, though. It was getting late and all I wanted was a shower. Shopping always made me feel sweaty. Then I would have a glass of wine and get into bed.

So rock and roll.

I couldn't wait to show off my new clothes, but it would have to wait until my next day off or an evening out. I wondered what Lou had been up to. He seemed to have done one of his vanishing acts again.

Chapter 23: Goodbye, sack of spuds!

'Morning! Wakey, wakey. Rise and shine!' Fran was hovering over me.

I opened one eye and looked at her, slightly dazed and confused as I had just woken up and was wondering what she was doing in my space.

'Er, morning!' I stretched out my arms and realised I hadn't set my alarm.

'Oh, what time is it?' I started to panic.

'It's nearly ten o'clock. I was starting to get worried about you as you're always up and at 'em. I thought I'd best come over and make sure you were OK.' She sat on one of the little camping chairs and waited for an explanation.

'Sorry, Fran, I forgot to set my alarm and just slept in. I can't understand it as I was in bed really early last night. Just give me a mo to get dressed and I'll be with you.' I wanted to get out of bed, but as I was naked I needed Fran to do one so I could get up.

'OK, as long as you're all right. I thought you might have done an all-nighter with Lou and Justin. They didn't come back last night, so I thought you might have been with them.' She got up and looked over at my bags of clothes.

'Been shopping?' She turned towards me with a smile.

'Yeah, I went yesterday.'

'About time, Annabel. You were looking like a sack of spuds, my darling.' She laughed and walked out.

She was absolutely right. Thanks to my parents, I had been able to get myself some new clothes and had even come away with some change. I had become a bit lax about contacting them, but I would ring them that night.

I also knew I really needed to start making plans for the future. Looking around me, reality was starting to bite. I couldn't stay at Sunnyside when the season finished. Although it had been my solace, I needed a plan B. I really wasn't sure what that plan could be.

I definitely wouldn't be going home; that wasn't even a plan B. I decided to think about it later, as I was already late for work. I didn't want to make my present situation a difficult one, as I was quite enjoying plan A for the time being.

Chapter 24: A shocking revelation

I arrived at the site office to find Justin sitting there looking smart in a suit and tie. He looked like he was going to a funeral, but he was still super hot. Somehow, suits and a tan with a blond-streaked barnet worked, and it made me look twice at him. Then I blushed, because I was getting quite aroused by the sight of him looking so dapper.

Justin was looking down at a set of notes. He was really concentrating and studying what was written on them. I wondered if he was preparing to give a speech at the funeral.

'Hello. Just picking up the Paulsons' and Joneses' keys to give their vans a scrub before they arrive today.' I directed this at Justin, as I felt I needed to say something to alert him to my presence.

'Oh, hi Annabel, you OK? Sorry, what did you say?' He looked up with a confused expression on his face.

'No worries. How are you? Everything OK?'

'Yes thanks. Well, I will be, I think. Got an interview in Milton Keynes later and I'm just doing some last-minute studying. When Mum picked me up from London we met up with one of her old contacts from her banking days and he's taking people on, but the job's in Singapore. I'd have to move there by October if I get it, which is, like, two months away.'

Rather than looking like at it as an opportunity of a lifetime, he was making the job sound like a life sentence.

'Wow, that's awesome! Sounds like a dream to me. How exciting! I've got five minutes, well kind of.

Shall I test you?' I wished it was me going. That would have been a great plan B!

'Nah, you're OK. To be honest, this interview is just a formality. It's my dad's company, so I kinda think I'll get the job. I pretty much know the company inside out. It's why my folks spilt up.' He smiled at me, but it was a forced, sad smile.

'Oh right, I see. I thought you said it was your mum's friend. But dude, this is an awesome opportunity, and it's being handed to you on a plate! Aren't you just a tad pleased?'

I crouched down and looked up at him.

'Annabel, there's so much you don't know. We call him a family friend, it's all very complicated. I feel like one stupid decision I made months ago has shaped my whole life.'

He looked at me and I saw his smouldering brown eyes looking straight into my soul. I hadn't seen him in such as intense mood before. He looked so timid and vulnerable that I wanted to sweep him into my arms and give him a cuddle.

'Is this about the girl in the village?' I stood up and sat on the arm of his chair.

'Yeah, the girl in the village. It's all about her and my stupid choice to take the...' He stopped himself.

'Take what? I know what you did. It happens all the time in cities, it's just because it's a small place that people gossip. I wouldn't beat yourself up about it. You were probably too young to be a dad and...'

'And what, Annabel? What do you know, hey? You haven't got a clue, have you?' he shot me a far less smouldering look and turned away.

'No, maybe I don't, but I know you were sent away because of it. You shouldn't beat yourself up about it. I'm sure you've learnt your lesson.'

'Learnt my lesson? Sorry, but who the fuck do you think you are? You have no idea! I was sent away for some shit I didn't do. I was helping out a mate because it's against his family's values and faith to get someone pregnant out of wedlock. And being a mate, I took the rap!'

He looked at me and then up at the ceiling, running his hands through his hair. 'Forget all that, I'm just stressed about this interview. Sorry for swearing at you, it was uncalled for.'

'So if you didn't get her pregnant, who did?' I sat there, thinking about the possibilities.

'Honestly, Annabel, leave it. Forget I said anything.' He sat back in the chair next to me and put a hand on my knee. 'Just forget it,' he said softly.

'But you've taken the fall for someone and that's not fair. Who would let you do that? Who would lt you be ostracised by the whole village for something you haven't done? Was it an old school friend? Oh, wait, I bet it's Scott from the pub.' I was going through every villager around Justin's age in my head.

'Was it Sam?' I continued. 'Oh, I bet it was Sam. He does look a bit smarmy. He's always talking to my boobs rather than my face.'

'Annabel, please leave it. It's over and done with now. I need to focus on today.' He started shuffling the papers in front of him.

'Oh my God! It was Lou, wasn't it?!' I had a sudden moment of realisation.

Of course it was Lou. He could charm the birds out the trees, and he was always very flippant whenever he mentioned Justin and the village girl, as if it was a joke or something insignificant.

I wrapped my arms around my head as if to give myself a hug.

'Justin, where does Lou keep disappearing to? Where is he right now?' I stood up with my hands on my hips.

He didn't respond.

'Justin, tell me. He hasn't been a good friend to you. Why do you keep protecting him?'

Justin put his head in his hands. 'Oh, Annabel. Why are you so frustrating? I asked you to leave it. Please just leave it, you don't understand.'

He put a hand on each of my shoulders and looked straight into my eyes. 'Please just leave it alone. What's done is done, we've all moved on.' He was firm but gentle.

'That doesn't answer my question. Where does Lou keep disappearing to? Tell me or I'll ask Fran!' I shook his hands off my shoulders.

'OK, I'll do you a deal. Let me go and do this interview and we'll talk this evening. We'll go to the pub. I just don't need this stress right now. Please promise me you'll hang fire and wait for me to come back. Please do this for me.'

He looked desperate and I didn't want to put any more stress on his shoulders. He had been through enough.

'OK, Justin. I'll wait till you get back, but if you don't tell me this evening I *will* ask Lou, then Fran, then the village girl. Understood?' I tried not to sound cross as I knew it wasn't his fault.

'Thanks, Annabel. Honestly, I'll tell you everything, as I think you deserve the truth.'

He kissed me on the forehead and cupped my face in his hands. 'I promise,' he whispered.

Chapter 25: Decision time

The day dragged by after my chat with Justin. I had so many questions I wanted to ask. I felt like I had been taken for a complete mug for the past couple of months. I had let someone into my life and trusted him with my most intimate feelings and thoughts, only to find out he was a lying, cheating fantasist who had been stringing me along. He probably thought fat Bella was so desperate she would shag anyone because she wouldn't get many other offers.

I stopped what I was doing and burst into tears. I felt like such an idiot.

Why did I always let myself be used? Why didn't I value myself more?

I had basically fallen for the first bit of flattery anyone had offered since Tim had dumped me.

I figured Lou was shacked up with his mystery woman, thinking he was getting a lucky break from the fat, desperate women I had become.

How had my life got so fucked up?

I decided it might be time ask my folks take me home. I could get myself a waitressing job in a teashop in town and save up some money until I figured out what to do with my messed-up life. My parents had probably been waiting for that phone call all this time.

But I had promised Justin I would wait until he got back before I made any decisions.

He had better have something honest and thought-provoking to say or I would be out of there, I thought to myself.

This made me cry even more, as I had enjoyed the best few months of my life at Sunnyside and had felt more at home than anywhere else, even my real home.

My campervan had been transformed from a shabby weed den into a hippy chick retreat, and I loved the change in my appearance. I looked healthier and slimmer; I hardly even recognised myself when I looked in the mirror. I just wished my taste in men wasn't so terrible. I always put everything into my relationships and fell so hard.

I had tried to hold back with Lou, pretending that I didn't really care where he was or what he was doing, but secretly I wanted to know where he was and why I was home alone all the time.

Maybe I was just too needy. I needed intimacy, reassurance and to be loved unconditionally. But how can you achieve unconditional love if you don't let yourself give and become 'one' in a relationship?

I had tried the too-cool-for-school approach and that obviously didn't work as it hadn't got me any further and I certainly didn't know the person I was supposedly with.

Chapter 26: In two minds

I felt irritable one minute and needy the next, so I tried to avoid contact with any of the residents and did my utmost to avoid the shed office, where Fran seemed to spend most of the day messing about with paperwork and looking flustered.

It was hard to stay incognito, though, as I was doing the gardening. I mainly had weeding to do as we had experienced a mixed bag of sunshine and showers, and the weeds were out in force. This meant I had to say hello to a lot more people that I would have liked to. In among them was Jude.

'Hey there, darlin', how are you? Where have you been holing up? Lou said he's been with you.' She threw me a coy smile.

'Oh yeah. Just chilling, Jude, just friendly like. Someone to hang about with who's the same age.'

Why was I lying? I hadn't seen him for days and neither had his mother, so why was I covering for him? I figured if I didn't I would blurt everything out and I didn't have all the facts yet. Oh, come on, Justin! Get home so I can stop my head exploding with malicious thoughts.

'Oh, sounds like a blast. Hope he's been a gentleman. You'll have to come and see us up in Wigan or join us on one of our trips to the States.'

She was drinking her morning coffee in the sun and looked so relaxed in her cream linen slacks and white shirt, which was blowing slightly in the wind. I really liked Jude. She was definitely my cup of tea, but it seemed as though she was always masking something more sinister.

Or maybe that was just my insecurities working overtime.

'That would be nice. Let me know when you're free,' I shouted over as I was walking over to another van to sort out the weed invasions there.

'Sure will,' she said with a wave.

I got my head down outside the Paulsons' van, hoping they wouldn't see me. I liked them, but they were a bit intense and I always had to watch what I was saying around them as I felt I was being analysed and judged.

'Morning, Annabel. You're later than usual. Did you have a late night?' Mrs Paulson asked quizzically.

I felt her gaze rest upon me as she waited for an answer.

'Morning. Sorry, hope it's not too late. I accidentally slept in.' I was hoping this answer would suffice.

'Oh yes, completely fine. There's nothing like the late part of the afternoon. I hope you get everything done.' She wandered back inside the van.

The exterior of their van was immaculate. Everything was just so, from the little pot plants on the decking to the outside lights, which came on as soon as dusk fell. The decking was scrubbed every other day, so it always looked new and tidy. I always wondered if their house was equally shipshape.

The weeding didn't take long. I was sure they had already been out, mortified at the fact that the garden looked less than pristine.

I went on to the Joneses' and McKenzies', and somehow managed to avoid eye contact with the owners. I seemed to be in the zone; I was like a weeding machine. I actually found it all quite therapeutic, as once I had cleared an area it looked lush.

I had got carried away and suddenly I felt a presence behind me. I turned to find Lou watching me.

'Hey, Annabel, where have you been hiding? I feel like I haven't seen you in ages. Come here, my little bundle of gorgeousness.'

He pulled me up, grabbed my face and slapped a massive kiss on my lips. I couldn't help but reciprocate, as it was just what I needed.

It was impossible to reject his lustful energy because it was always so powerful and it made me feel like I was the only one on his radar. He knew where to touch and where to put his hands and lips. He pressed me against the van with my hands held above my head and worked his lips down my neck and onto my chest. I felt my breaths getting deeper. I yanked my arms down and pulled him up off his knees.

'Lou, not here or now,' I scolded him.

'Come on, Annabel. No one's around, and look who's pleased to see you, as always.' He brushed his huge hard-on against my bare thigh. I could have just taken him there and then, but I was still confused and angry about what I had found out that morning.

'I'll meet you at your van in ten minutes. I'll be waiting for you, sweetheart.' He gave me a long, lingering kiss and placed my hand on his cock.

I started to get wet. *Maybe I could just have one last fumble; use him like he had been using me.*

He walked off in the direction of my van looking as hot as he always did in cut-off, mid-length denim shorts, a low V-necked T-shirt and flip-flops.

I spent the next ten minutes battling with my conscience.

Should I wait for Justin to get back and find out the facts, or should I just go with my feelings right now? Or should I ask Lou directly what had been going on; why he had been so aloof one minute and the love of my life the next? He never explained his absences. He just left me without a word and then turned up again, full of charm and expecting me to fall in line.

I felt my need for sex was starting to outweigh the more sensible options. I was all worked up having felt how hard he was. He was probably in my van wanking that great big cock and waiting for me to slip on top of him to slowly make up for days of lost time.

Grrrrrr! Ohhhh, what should I do?

I gripped at my hair like a mad woman. I felt as though I was being split in two.

Chapter 27: Murder afoot!

At that moment, Jude came round the corner. 'Hey there, honey. What's going on? Are you OK?' She placed a gentle hand on my shoulder.

I felt like I was going slightly insane. I wanted to blurt it all out and let someone else figure out what to do, but obviously I was too soft and decent to start bombarding Lou's mother about the whats, whys and wherefores of her son.

"Oh, hi Jude. No, everything's fine. I just nearly stood on Mrs Paulson's lilac bush and you know how she likes a tidy bush.'

I hadn't meant that to sound the way it did, but to be fair Mrs Paulson was quite particular.

'Oh sure, honey. But I don't think it's worth you getting upset about. I'm sure she'll understand.' Jude was looking at me with such kindness.

I really liked this woman and wanted to reach out to her.

'Have you seen Fran around? She seems to be very hard to find of late. It's ever since you've been around. I guess that's what she's paying you for, but I kinda wonder what the point is...'

She looked away and rapidly changed the subject. "Are you around this evening? Lou and I have to go to Wigan tomorrow and then to the States. We've got some business to take care of. I think Lucas is on about opening a subsidiary in Singapore.'

She always looked relieved at the thought of leaving the site. I could understand that the prospect of going to the States was far more appealing than staying at Sunnyside. It was still a mystery to me as to why they had ever started coming here.

'Sure, I haven't got any other plans,' I said, adding, silently in my head ...*apart from finding out why your son is as elusive as the Scarlet Pimpernel and why he let his mate take the fall for some girl's 'forced' abortion.*

'Oh good. If the weather holds and we don't get any thunderstorms, I'll do a barbecue with some wine. Can you pass the message on to Fran, please? If she shows up today...'

Jude looked a little miffed, but she was right. I hardly saw Fran around these days. I laid eyes on her about once a week, which was bizarre as she lived and worked on the site. If I didn't get to see her, my wages would be left on the table in the office. I wondered whether Justin's arrival had unnerved her a little and she felt it was best to lie low.

I had so many questions and there was nobody around to answer them. I felt like I was stuck in the middle of a whodunit novel.

Someone would be murdered before the day was out!

Chapter 28: Time for some answers

I only had one more van to do, but I was starting to lose the will to live and my patience was running low. Justin should surely be back soon. Lou was nowhere to be seen after he had disappeared more than two hours earlier, but that was no surprise as I had said I would only be ten minutes. He hadn't even come to try and win me over, which wasn't like Lou. He was like a dog in heat half the time.

I decided to call it a day. I was sure the weeds weren't going to do a disappearing act and my head was all over the place. I needed a shower and then I would wait for Justin to return from bloody Milton Keynes.

I got to the van and found the door wide open.

'You could have shut the door, Lou!' I mumbled to myself.

He was so thoughtless; he didn't have a care for anyone but himself.

I got through the door and saw Justin flaked out on the sofa. I felt relieved to see him and instantly became less restless. I decided to take a shower so I felt clean before my quest to find out why everyone had been lying to me began.

Chapter 29: The 'truth' revealed

By the time I returned from the shower room, Justin was sitting up on the sofa trying to tune in the tiny portable telly.

'You'll never do it, I've been trying for months. You might get a little glimpse of something, but then it goes.'

I was secretly hoping he would get a picture as I was missing a bit of telly.

'Oh Bell, you scared the crap out of me! Where have you been? I've been here for hours!'

'I've been at work and when I got back you were fast asleep, so I thought I'd get a shower and clear my head. Are you ready to explain what's been going on or shall I go straight to Lou? I've already seen him today, by the way, but I kept my mouth shut.'

I was determined to be forthright as I didn't want to hear any more bull.

Just as I started talking, the heavens opened and it rained like I had never seen since I had been in the van. It made an awful noise on the roof, as if a million wildebeest were stampeding across it.

I closed the door as some of the drips were starting to waft in with the wind.

'Well, I got the job,' Justin said as an opener.

'Sorry, you got robbed?' I couldn't make out what he was saying as the rain was so loud.

'No! I got the job and I leave in September for some initial training. My father's going to take me over and spend some time with me over there.' He was shouting over the noise of the rain.

'Oh great, that sounds good,' I said, although I hadn't heard much apart from September.

'Yeah, my father's decided I'm just as important as Lou and deserve to be treated as such, and not like a mistake.'

He looked adorable as he played with his hair and gazed down at the floor.

'That's so cool. I'm glad Lou's important to you. I guess that's why you've taken the rap, but you really need to start telling everyone.' I was finding this conversation exhausting with all the shouting involved.

'So Jude and my father are moving back to the States after we've sorted out the Singapore branch and by the end of the year Lou's gonna join them. Mum's gonna sell the park and go travelling. They've decided me taking the fall for my "little bro" wasn't the wisest plan of all time, but once we're away from this place we can all move on.' He looked at me and smiled. 'See, all sorted. There's nothing to worry about.'

'Oh right, so you're moving to the States with Lou and your mum's moving to Wigan with Jude and Lucas? It all seems a little cosy, but hey, it doesn't get any cosier than this site.'

It all sounded quite bizarre based on what I thought I had heard, but then none of them seemed quite normal anyhow.

The rain on the roof suddenly ended and my ears stopped ringing.

'So when are you going to start packing?' I shouted without realising.

'Hey, I'm only over here,' he said, smiling cheekily.

'Sorry, that was one hell of a storm.'

I was looking up, pointing out the obvious. 'Anyway, never mind where everyone's heading off to in the next few months, I want to know where Lou's been sloping off to recently.'

'Hey, did someone say my name?' Lou opened the door with the usual smirk plastered all over his face.

'Erm, no. You're hearing things, bro,' Justin said.

I always found the way they called each other bro quite cute.

'I was wondering...'

As I started talking, Justin stood up and spoke over me. 'We were wondering if you're up for a drink, either here or at the pub. I've finally got the old man to give me a step up.' He nudged Lou.

'High five, dude. That's awesome, I can't believe it. When are you leaving?'

They high-fived and I felt a bit left out.

'Well, the old dude's going over and getting the handover sorted, then I'm gonna fly over in a week or so and sign on the dotted line.' Justin looked pleased and relieved.

'Cool, he's been wanting to do this for so long. It'll be great for you both. How does Fran feel about it?' Lou asked, looking a little concerned.

'She's OK. I think she'll be glad to get rid of the noose around her neck that's been holding her back for so long. It's time she did what she wants for a change.'

He helped himself and Lou to a drink. 'Do you want wine or beer, Bella?'

'I'll have a beer, please. I feel like I need one.'

I sat down with Lou on one side and Justin on the other. It felt very weird, but awfully nice. For some reason, Justin clearly didn't want me to confront Lou and it was starting to bug me.

I only wanted to ask one simple question: *Where the hell do you keep disappearing to?*

I was completely confused and felt as though I was more in the dark than ever; like I was being talked around and not told the truth.

Was I missing something?

Chapter 30: No means no

I was on my third pint and fifth toilet trip when Lou appeared in the shower block, waiting for me.

'Hey you, got you alone at last. Justin can be quite boring, can't he? Come here and give me some love.'

He looked at me in his normal frisky way, but this time his smouldering good looks and fine body weren't doing anything for me. I felt he was hiding something and Justin was covering for him.

I was getting used just for sex whenever he felt the need to offload. He didn't give me any real emotional support. We didn't have nice meals out or go to the cinema. It was just a quickie here and there, or a picnic near the canal, which ultimately ended in sex.

'We should get back to Justin.'

I tried to move past him, but he grabbed me by the waist.

'Hey, where do you think you're going?' he asked, looking down at his dick.

I felt my guts churn over and finally saw him for what he was: a spoilt, overprotected brat who was used to getting everything, and everyone, the way he wanted.

'I'm going back to the van to have a drink with Justin,' I said in such a stern manner he was forced to take note of what I was saying.

'What's up with you? Come on, he'll be OK for five minutes.'

'Oh, five minutes just so you can get your end away and go. Well, I don't know where you go.' My arms started to do the talking as I flung them around.

'What's got your goat? You've never complained before. You seemed quite happy having your first multiple. You know what they say... once you've had a bit of Lou you never go back.' He looked so sure of himself.

'Well I've decided that I don't want a bit of Lou, and I'm quite happy never to go back.'

I looked him straight the eye, struggling to believe I had fallen for this dick so soon after Tim.

'Oh well, you go and have a shandy with Justin and I'll go and get my pleasure from Kate. I'm sure she won't mind getting a multiple tonight.' He lent against the wall and crossed his arms and legs.

'Oh Kate... the girl you made Justin take the blame for because he "forced" her to have an abortion when all the time it was you!'

I knew I was raising my voice, and I hated the fact that I was doing so because, as they say, once you've raised your voice you've lost the argument.

Lou stood there for a moment as if he was looking for the right words, but instead he chose to say: 'Yeah, well she's still gagging for a bit of Lou cock, and when I can't find you I give it to her.' And with that he walked out.

'For goodness' sake, Lou, grow up! You can't keep going around thinking you're God's gift, getting girls pregnant and then asking your "best mate" to take the rap.'

I was getting fed up with his arrogant attitude towards women.

'Hey, it wasn't my fault. I thought she was seventeen. She never told me she was just a girl and I'd already had a caution for assault, so I needed my bro to handle it.' He held his hands up in defence.

'Oh my God! "Girl" was a just a term I was using to describe her. I didn't realise she was underage! How *could* you?'

He tried to grab me again, but I pulled away. I opened the door to leave as I didn't want to be in his presence a moment longer.

'Your loss, Bella. See you around. It was fun while it lasted.' He blew me a kiss and trotted off, just as he had done on numerous other occasions.

I wasn't sure how to feel. I finally had the answer I had been looking for, but I felt so used and empty, and slightly dirty knowing he had been going back and forth between me and Kate in the village.

Because everyone thought Justin was the black sheep, Lou got away with sleeping around without detection as he was only in the area intermittently.

I had only been in lust with him, so all I had wanted was his passion, but as my feelings started to get deeper, he must have known that questions regarding his whereabouts would be asked.

Chapter 31: Good riddance

I made my way back to the van feeling physically and emotionally drained.

How could anyone be so thoughtless in regard to other people's feelings?

I was also cross with myself for getting emotionally involved with someone like him. I had been taken over by the flattery and he had finally made me feel worthy again.

Maybe people like Lou had their place in society: to help mend broken hearts but also to make them wiser about the people they shouldn't let into their lives.

I was just glad I could hold my head up high and move on, which brought me back to making plans for another slice of life.

When I got back to the van, Justin was still there. I had half-thought he might have disappeared.

'Hey, did Lou catch up with you?' He looked at me with suggestively raised eyebrows.

'Yeah, he did, and quite frankly he gives me the creeps. I know what you did for him and why, and it's very noble of you, but you mustn't feel like you bear that tag any more. Release yourself from the past and look forward to the future.'

I was very pleased with my deep and meaningful speech. I turned to Justin and smiled.

'Woah, Bell, that's a bit deep. Don't worry, I think those shackles are off now. I think Dad's seen the light, and now he knows the truth he feels bad for sending me packing. Mum never likes to rock the boat, so she just went along with it.' He looked a lot happier and more relaxed than he had earlier that morning.

'Was it good to see your dad after all this time?' I sat next to him and put my right hand on his knee.

'Well, I saw him in a different capacity, I guess. He was in a suit and tie, and was surrounded by yes men… but then Jude was bugging him to go to the "mall" every spare minute, as usual.' He was mid-speech when something twigged in my brain.

'Wait a minute… Lucas is your dad?' I felt thoroughly confused.

'Erm, yeah, I told you all this earlier. Weren't you listening? Or were you too interested in lover boy?' It was his turn to look miffed.

'No, I couldn't hear a word you were saying. All I heard was that you were moving to Wigan or someone was. What, so Lucas is your dad and Lou is your stepbrother? So that means… Oh, Fran and Lucas… Oh my word!' I put my hand over my mouth.

'Hello! Yes! Fran and my dad were having an affair. They reckon it was over and done with before Lou was even a twinkle in Jude's eye. She didn't seem that bothered about it. Why do you think they come here, of all the places they could go? It isn't for the weather or the location, however pretty it is.'

The more he talked, the more my questions were being answered. It made sense that Lucas and Jude came, and that Jude and Fran were sometimes ill at ease with one another. I had always thought it a little odd that they chose to spend their holidays at Sunnyside.

The Singapore job offer seemed to be Lucas' olive branch to Justin for not giving him all the advantages in life Lou had received, and not just because of the Kate situation.

It just showed how boys with virtually the same blood could be treated in such different ways, with such different results. Justin was respectful and kind, while Lou was just a dick on legs, and a spoilt dick at that.

'So how come your mum ended up here at the caravan park?' I was starting to put the jigsaw puzzle together in my head.

'Mum's originally from Bradbury, but she moved away and did the uni thing. She got a job as a PA, met Lucas, got up the duff and was paid to keep quiet. She found a caravan site for sale, and that was that. Lucas gave my mum the money to get the site up and running, and she was happy as Larry. She rarely went anywhere, but she always brought me up to be kind and respectful.'

He smiled and then continued. 'I saw my dad a lot, but I wasn't introduced to him as his son. They were just Jude and Lucas, and once Lou was born we became inseparable. We were sort of brought up as brothers when they were around, which is ironic, I know, but it all worked out and everyone managed and got on well. It was only when Lou started to think with his groin that things started to go a little pear-shaped.'

'Well, onwards and upwards, I suppose. You have your posh new job in Singapore, and you're doing well whatever you'll be doing out there. It'll be great. A fresh start and all that.'

I was so envious. *I wished my super rich dad would turn up and give me a lifeline... not that my folks hadn't helped me out.*

'What are you gonna do, Bell? What are your plans for after the summer, or will you stay on? Maybe you could move into Lucas and Jude's van. They'll be moving soon, so it'll be empty.'

I realised this was part of the conversation I had missed in the rain. 'Oh, where are they going?' I said quietly as I didn't want him to think I hadn't been listening at all.

'Back to the States. Jude feels it's the right time. She feels we've all made amends and are ready to move on without feeling obliged to stay in the UK. Shall I ask them about the van for you?'

He looked excited and it clearly gave him joy to think that he was helping me out.

'No, ta. I really need to make amends with myself and move on; get a life or a job somewhere. I'm not entirely sure where. If nothing pans out, I'll move back to my folks' place for a while as I'm running out of other options. I've had a great summer, and the drama has added to the enjoyment!'

I was smiling, as it really had been great. Even the fling with Lou and how it had ended hadn't been awful. In fact, I had enjoyed it a lot while it lasted!

'OK, just give me five and I'll be back. I need a quick shower and a change of clothes.' He dashed off.

It was getting a bit nippy, so I put a jumper on and cuddled up under the duvet, just for a few minutes. It was getting dark and I was shattered. The day's events and revelations had taken it out of me, as had the beers. It wasn't long before I was fast asleep.

Chapter 32: Facing the future

I was awoken by the normal morning chorus of birds singing and I could hear someone out mowing their own lawn, which was music to my ears as it would save me a job. It was my day off and I fully intended to make the most of it. I really needed my new plan A to be a good one.

A trip to the job centre was in order to see whether there were any opportunities that looked suitable. I felt my stint in the navy and my summer of grafting in the mud would stand me in good stead.

The nearest job centre was in a nearby town called Shilton. I had never needed to go there before. I had been quite happy pottering around Bradbury except for my single shopping excursion to Nottingham.

Shilton was a market town with a pedestrianised centre containing numerous shops, banks and the obligatory charity shops. The bus took me straight into the heart of the town and the job centre was only a few minutes' walk away.

I had asked the bus driver how to get there and he had said, 'It's that way, me duck,' pointing towards the front of the bus. 'Then turn up Ashley Street and it's up there, ducky,' he had added.

I had nodded thanks and waved goodbye. I wasn't used to being called duck. I found it quite funny and I heard myself say 'quack quack' in my head.

I eventually found the job centre after a few more queries, as the bus driver hadn't given me the most accurate of directions. The outside looked as interesting as the inside. There were various tables with advisers sitting behind them and lots of telephone stations for people to ring potential employers.

There was nothing for it but to ask for help. I felt like going in and saying, 'SOS! Please help me get a life, a job… anything!'

I tried to stay calm, as I could feel myself getting agitated at the thought of not knowing what my future would hold. Five months earlier I had been embarking on a fresh start with the love of my life, and now I was at the job centre wondering what the hell I was going to do with my life.

'Hi, can I help?' A friendly face looked up at me from a nearby desk.

'Oh, yes please. I really do need help.' I hadn't meant to sound so desperate.

'Come and have a seat, me duck.'

There it was again… quack quack.

'Thanks.' I sat down opposite a lovely looking lady, who might have been old enough to be my gran or young enough to be my mother. She had short, greying blonde hair and wore rimless glasses and colourful beads. I noticed these as I liked them, and I had a new dress they would have looked awesome with.

'So what do we call you? Can I take some details for the system?' Her fingers were poised and ready on the keyboard.

'Yes, my name's Annabel McClintock. I'm twenty-four and have no fixed address.' That part made me feel sick.

'OK, Annabel. Are you selling *The Big Issue* or are you affiliated with any charities?' she asked kindly.

'Oh no, sorry. I'm not homeless. I live in Bradbury on the caravan site. What I meant was, I'll be moving on soon. And no, I'm not a traveller, either!'

I giggled as it all sounded so bizarre.

Gill giggled too. I noticed that her name badge said 'Employment supervisor', so I was hoping I had found the right lady.

'OK, so can you give me your temporary address just for the records? And a phone number?'

'Yes, it's Sunnyside Caravan Park, Bradbury Road, Bradbury. Sorry, I'm not sure what the postcode is, and I don't remember the phone number.'

I wasn't a fan of mobiles, they seemed so intrusive, and I didn't want to give them the office number as I wanted to keep my plans from Fran for the time being in case nothing came up.

'Lovely. Right, let's take some details of your experience. Where have you worked before and for how long?'

'That's the easy bit. I joined the navy when I was nineteen and left when I was twenty-two. I was unemployed till about five months ago, when I got a job at the caravan park as a kind of maintainer, gardener, cleaner kind of person,' I said very matter-of-factly, as if nothing could be simpler.

'Wow, you were in the navy? What did you do?' Gill looked genuinely interested.

'I was a radar operator and weapons' mechanic. And when I was shore-based for a while I worked as a PA for a lieutenant.' Even I thought this sounded impressive.

'So you're adaptable to a multitude of environments, you have a willingness to learn. You can take instructions and enjoy a challenge, and you have office-based skills.' She nodded over at me, willing me to agree.

'Erm, yes. All those things, I guess.'

'And you like new challenges and enjoy being outdoors.'

She was tapping away at her computer as she spoke.

She was making me sound like the most employable person in the job centre and I was starting to build up a bit of confidence. I had always shrugged off my time in the navy as I hadn't particularly enjoyed it and hadn't done it for very long, so I had always felt like a bit of a failure.

I usually tried to shrug it off as just a 'thing' I had done, but I don't suppose many people have sat at a desk watching blips, making sure the navigation officer didn't crash into them by sending him situation reports, while living at sea for months on end and not seeing anyone apart from the ship's company.

I had needed to be on my best behaviour as I ate, slept and lived with them around the clock, and there was nowhere to hide. I had enjoyed playing volleyball on the flight deck and doing circuits round the ship. And when we hit shore it had been so much fun; it was like letting a bunch of caged animals out on the prowl.

It made me quite sad to think about it, as I had blocked it all out for so long. There had been good times, but I had been so in love with Tim that when he had been made redundant I had just wanted to leave. I had felt so alone in Portsmouth without him. I was on the ship and he was on shore, so I had been able to see him when I had a day off or when we got shore leave, but it wasn't the same.

I felt sad that I had put Tim before my career. I really wished I would learn to let my head rule my heart and not the other way around.

'Right then, Annabel. Here's an up-to-date CV. I suggest you go on the computer over there, enter some details and see what jobs might be right for you. Take note of the location. If you're not bothered where you live, you may find more job opportunities open to you.'

Gill passed me a piece of paper with my CV on it. As I read it, I was convinced it was about someone else. I sounded like an ambitious, dynamic young woman. I liked the sound of that and was determined to make Gill proud.

Chapter 33: In demand

The job search wasn't going to plan. Every single job service-type job came up, including the police, fire brigade, prison service and even the RSPCA, probably because its staff wore a uniform.

I wasn't interested in doing anything of the sort. That was the old Annabel. I wanted a new me and a new life.

'Argh, this is hopeless!' I let out a sigh and the people sitting either side of me looked at me as if was a loon.

I decided to get myself home. I had been at the job centre all afternoon and it was starting to depress me. I was no further forward, apart from having a piece of paper that made me sound great.

Once again, I was beginning to think I would need to phone my parents to see if my dad could pick me up and whether they would let me stay for a couple of months until I got myself sorted.

I felt my heart sink as I stood at the bus stop. I had been full of hope that morning and had been really determined to sort my life out without resorting to phoning my mum, but maybe it was time to admit defeat.

I got back to the park after taking a short walk along the canal to clear my head. It was a little nippy, but I was walking at a healthy pace so I didn't feel it. As I headed back to my van I bumped into a flustered Fran.

'Have you seen Justin?' She grabbed the tops of my arms as if her life depended on the answer.

'No, why?' I stopped dead in my tracks.

'Oh, he's been looking for you all day. Where have you been?' She looked a tad wild, but I could see that she was happy about something.

'I went to Shilton. I needed to go to the bank.' I had to lie as I didn't want to say I had been at the job centre.

"OK, well stay in your van and I'll go and find him.'

She literally ran off in search of her son.

What on earth is going on? Has he discovered the meaning of life? I wondered.

Chapter 34: Life-changing news

I really needed a shower, as I felt a little grubby after being out in town all afternoon. I hated touching door handles in public places; even the thought of it made me shudder.

I decided to nip in while Fran ran around the caravan park looking for Justin.

It was piping hot, which was just what I needed. I sat on the shower tray and just let the water fall on me. I had my head in my hands and suddenly I was crying. I felt like such a failure. I had no formal education, apart from a few GCSEs and very little relevant work experience. The only jobs out there seemed to be office or shop-based.

It made me so jealous that Tim, who I had left my career for, was enjoying his new opportunity in the prison service with a stack of money behind him and without a care or a thought as to where I was or what I was up to. I bet he thought I had just rung my parents and that I was sponging off them.

I still couldn't believe the way he had walked out of my life and never, in all these months, been in contact to see if I was OK, or if I was even still around. I suppose some people are just selfish.

As long as they were getting what they wanted out of life, fuck everyone else.

I still had my suspicions that he had been seeing someone else, as it seemed to have been a little too easy for him to dump me the way he had.

The water started to get cold and I could still feel the tears rolling down my face. I had never felt so lonely and depressed. I just didn't know what to do.

'Annabel, Annabel! Are you in there?' I heard Justin shout through the door.

'Yes, what's going on? What's the emergency?'

Can't I even have a shower and wallow in self-pity any more? I thought to myself.

'Hurry up, I've got something to tell you. I've been looking for you all day!' He sounded excited.

I guessed he wanted to tell me when his flight was leaving.

Whoopie do for you, Justin. Let me drag my arse out of this hot shower, dry my tears and then you can tell me your exciting fucking news!

'Just give me a minute and I'll be out.' I couldn't have sounded less impressed if I had tried.

I wandered back to my van to be joined by Justin, Fran, Jude and Lucas. And although I didn't realise it straight away, my mum and dad were standing right at the back.

'Okkkkk, what's going on? Have I missed my birthday or something? I'm pretty sure that's not till March...' I felt utterly confused.

'No, it's even better than that!' Justin said enthusiastically.

'Did you have any joy at the job centre, Annabel?' Fran asked with a gentle smile.

I turned bright red.

How on earth did she know I had been at the job centre?

'Small towns,' Fran said, as if she had read my mind.

'Oh, not so well. Sorry... It's not that I'm not happy, I've had the best time, but...' I was talking way too fast to make any sense.

"It's OK, chutney, you don't need to explain. Lucas has a proposition for you, and Fran called us in case it's not what you want, as we all think you've had a rough few months and need some time out.' My dad was sitting, cuppa in hand, with a look of concern on his face.

I hadn't realised I had been acting so desperate. It irritated me a little that everyone thought they knew me better than I knew myself.

'OK, so, as you know, Justin is leaving for Singapore soon,' said Lucas.

Oh great, thanks for the reminder. Next you're going to ask me if I can caravan sit for you until next summer.

'Well, we've been having a chat and we need someone we can trust to go over with Justin to help with his admin. There's a PA position on offer if you want it?' Jude said, linking arms with her husband.

'So what do you think? Why do you think I've been looking for you all day?' Justin looked like he was about to explode with excitement.

I didn't know what to do or say, but I knew I needed to sit down, and quickly.

'That sounds utterly amazing, but I've never done anything like that before.'

There I was, like clockwork, putting myself down and out of the game.

'Well, that isn't what your CV says. It says right here you were PA to a lieutenant in the navy.'

Lucas held up a copy my CV. I had no idea where he had got it from.

'Oh yeah, I did a few months in the office. But that was a long time ago, and, well...' I started to stutter as everyone was just staring at me.

'Annabel, you've been handed a golden opportunity,' said Lucas. 'I've chatted with your parents at length about it. We'll make sure you have an apartment all paid for by the company and a year's contract. If you prove your worth and loyalty, we'll re-evaluate your future after that.'

I looked at my parents and my dad was giving me a knowing nod; a nod that was urging me to go for it. Mum was welling up, I wasn't sure why. Maybe they were happy tears as it meant I wouldn't be going back to their house to mess up her cleaning and socialising routines.

I took a massive gulp and blurted out: 'Yes! Yes please! That sounds amazing!'

And it truly did.

Justin ran over to me and gave me a huge congratulatory hug. 'We'll make a great team,' he said softly.

I felt completely overwhelmed.

Fifteen minutes earlier I had been crying rivers of self-pity tears in the shower and now I had bagged myself a job in bloody Singapore. I mean, OMG! I was off to Singapore!

It was all starting to dawn on me.

My parents came over and gave me a kiss and a cuddle. I felt so grateful that they cared about me. I hated all the emotional stuff, but I always knew that, if push came to shove, the two people hugging the crap out of me were my rock. If my dad had shaken his head, Singapore would have been out of the water; that's how much I trusted his judgement.

But somehow this felt right. This was why Tim had dropped me here. This was why he had left without looking back. Fate had led me to this path.

'If it doesn't work out, you're only a flight away,' my dad said. 'Take the opportunity you've been given and embrace it.'

He always had the right thing to say at the right time.

'We're going to miss you, chipmunk, but you must do what's best for you,' my mum said, squeezing my forearms tightly.

I walked over to Lucas. 'Thank you so much. This has come at such a good time in my life. I wasn't sure what I was going to do, but this job, this opportunity, has fallen so right for me. I really appreciate you thinking of me.' I felt a wave of emotion entering my voice.

'Annabel, I've met all kinds of people in my lifetime, and I know when I meet a genuine person who just needs a bit of luck. It seems you've given plenty of other people a leg up, so I'm giving you one.'

Fran appeared with champagne and glasses, and she had a massive grin on her face. She looked more relaxed than she had been of late. She was probably glad all the hiding out from the villagers was over. This would be a fresh start for all of us.

They all started chatting about the weather and tennis, but I just listened and thought about how lucky I was. I hadn't known most of these people long, but they had found it in them to offer me the chance of a lifetime.

I looked over at the weeping willow curtain and saw that it was being pushed aside. Through it walked Lou followed by a glowing woman, who I assumed must be Kate!

I didn't know where to look as I was just gawping. They looked like newlyweds; really loved up. It made me kind of angry, as Kate seemed to be enjoying Lou's doormat treatment.

'Hey guys, I wondered where you all were. We've been looking for you both,' he said, focusing on Jude and Lucas.

'Well now you've found us,' replied Lucas, who appeared less than interested in what his son had to say.

'Well, we'd like you all to be the first to congratulate us on our news. Kate and I are going to be parents, and to make it all legitimate we decided to hotfoot it to Gretna Green yesterday and get hitched.'

He held up Kate's hand, which was decorated with a small but impressive rock and band. Then he proudly held up a baby scan picture.

'This time no one can disrupt our happiness. It's all above board.'

Like a true gentleman, Justin walked over and shook his hand, congratulating them both.

Jude completely lost her cool. 'You've done what? After everything you've put this family through! You just don't learn, do you Lou? You don't have any self-control! You've been treating Annabel like a mattress... sorry Annabel.'

She looked at me and winced as she realised she had dropped me in it with my folks.

'...And now you turn up with the girl we tried to protect, and you tell us she's pregnant again... and that you've gone and got married. I just don't get you!' She stormed off, with Lucas in tow.

'Let's get this party started,' said Lou without flinching.

'Hang on a second. This party is nothing to do with you. I'm pleased you've made a decision that isn't entirely based on your self-centred, egotistical ways, but this party is a celebration of something you're not part of, and that's Annabel's happiness and future. So no disrespect to you or Kate, but can you leave so we can get the party started without you?'

Justin was displaying the manliest side I had ever seen in him. He was full of rage but expressed it in a controlled manner.

He turned his back on Lou and offered me some more champagne.

'You're just jealous,' Lou retorted.

'Sorry? Why am I jealous, exactly? Pray tell!'

'You've always been stuck here under Fran's shadow, scared of going anywhere or doing anything for fear my father would cut you out of his life completely. I can't believe how pathetic you were, looking forward to his summer visits down here while I was having all the fun of the fair, including old Annabel over there. I bet you wish it was you that…'

And with that, there was a loud smack, and Lou went down like a sack of spuds.

My dad stood holding his hand as he addressed Lou. 'A word to the wise, son. If you're going to use my daughter like a doormat, make sure I'm not within hitting distance! Now clear off and find the rock you can't get out from under, 'cause if I clap eyes on you again I'll give you more than just a smack around the mouth.'

Lou opened his mouth to say something, but thought better of it. He grabbed poor Kate's hand and disappeared through the willow tree.

'What on earth was he expecting? Did he think we would all sit around romancing about how it's all turned out great, and what an amazing guy he is for getting the girl pregnant but agreeing to marry her and make it all fabulous?' said Justin.

He sat in the deck chair next to mine.

We clinked glasses and he said, 'To us. To Singapore!'

I repeated the words of the toast with gusto.

My parents had arranged with the Paulsons to stay in their van for a couple of nights, so they headed back there to turn in. I was glad they were staying as I wanted to spend the following day with them to discuss the future.

But right at that moment I was quite happy looking up at the sky with Justin by my side. I felt as was as though it was the first day of the rest of my life. It was a superb plan A.

Chapter 35: Closure

I had just about managed to get myself to bed, a little tipsy after Justin and I had decided to open a bottle of Jack Daniels. I wasn't too keen on it usually, but after a few drinks it didn't take much to twist my arm, especially when it came to alcohol and knocking more of it back. I woke up feeling a little worse for wear.

If I had remembered rightly, Justin would be leaving for Singapore in a couple of days and had said that I should do the same, as it would be good to find our feet together around the city before hitting the grind.

I had a quick shower, as I wanted to see Fran first thing. She seemed to have disappeared the night before, just after the champagne had run out. I wanted to officially hand in my notice, and to thank her taking me in, giving me a job and a home, and for helping me believe in myself again.

I wandered over to the office and found a very hungover Fran slumped over the desk.

'Morning, Fran. You OK?' I put my hand on her shoulder and gave it a gentle shove.

'Urgh! Morning, Annabel. How are you? I feel like my head's going to explode.'

She didn't get up or even raise her head off the table.

'Do you want some paracetamol or water?' I asked as I sat on the fold-up chair next to her.

'No, darling, just leave me be for a while. I should be OK by about... never.' She looked up and gave me a wry smile. 'So how did the celebrating go?'

'Obviously not as well as yours!'

We both giggled.

'I'm so pleased for you,' she said. 'Pleased everything's turning out so great. You deserve it after that shitbag Tim left you here like he did. Oh, speaking of Tim, he dropped by a couple of days ago and left you a letter.' She pointed towards my inbox tray.

'When? He left a note and you didn't you tell me?' I searched through my inbox until I found the letter. I could recognise his handwriting a mile off, as it looked like a doctor's scrawl.

I opened it and it read:

Dear Annabel,

Sorry I've only just managed to put pen to paper so I can try to explain or justify my actions towards you. In a way, it was because of my love for you that I did what I did. We had become more like brother and sister than lovers. I hadn't felt like we were a couple for a long time. I was hoping you felt the same, but I just didn't have the guts to confront you. When I took the prison job I was hoping it would be a fresh start for me, and not for us, so that's why I just bolted.

I knew you weren't far away from your parents, and I knew deep down you didn't really want me; you were in love with the thought of me. I'd been your safety blanket for a long time and I thought without me you'd grow into someone different.

We weren't on the same page any more. We'd moved on and grown up, and grown out of each other.

I've met someone new, but that wasn't intentional or premeditated, it just happened. I wanted to know you were happy and secure and not miserable or waiting around for me. I know now after to speaking to Fran that you've blossomed, and that makes me so happy. I knew you never would have done so if we had stayed together; it was me holding you back.

Grab life with both hands!

I will always love and care for you, and will always have your best interests at heart.

Please forgive me for leaving you that day, but it was because I loved you and knew that being together would destroy us eventually. I would rather have left you hurt than broken.

I wish you all the very best in Singapore, Fran mentioned told me. I remember you always wanted to go there after watching Rogue Trader *because you fancied Ewan McGregor!*

Always be the true you.

Love

Tim

By the time I had finished reading, I was in floods of tears. I just sat there weeping as everything he had said in the letter was so true.

We had stopped being lovers. We had been in love, but not in the kind of way that lasts forever. He had done me a favour, but I couldn't help but miss him. He had been the only constant thing in my life for a long time. But it was time to lay my past to rest.

I found some matches, lit the bottom corner of the letter and watched my past burn away.

'Didn't like what he wrote? Fran piped up.

'To the contrary, I agreed with everything he said. I just don't need to read it all again; I got it the first time.' I wiped my tears away.

These were the last tears I would ever cry for Tim.

'Oh good. He seemed really cut up when he dropped by.'

'Yeah, talking about that, why didn't you tell me?' I felt a little conspired against.

'I did it when the time was right.' She lifted a finger and pointed to the sky.

'Thanks, Fran. And thank you for taking a punt on me. I'm not sure what I'd have done without

Sunnyside and you.' I wanted to hug her, but she had started snoring.

I decided to pop over to the Paulsons' caravan for a brew with my parents.

I wouldn't mention Tim or the letter; there wasn't any point.

Chapter 37: A new life beckons

Leaving day came around far too quickly. I was starting to wonder whether I had done the right thing, but Jude and Lucas were very supportive, and my parents helped me pack. We had even taken a shopping trip into Nottingham to get some more business-like attire.

It was all starting to feel real. Lucas had sorted the visas and had rented a couple of one-bedroom apartments next to each other in the city. It made me feel safer knowing that Justin would be just next door. I knew I would be working with him every day, but being somewhere completely new it was comforting to know that he would be in the next flat.

We hadn't had much time to chat about the flight, the job or the new country, but I was guessing Justin was as nervous as I was. He had the added pressure of not wanting to disappoint his dad, whereas I would just be told what to do and get on with it.

My parents wanted to stay until it was time to go to the airport, as they wanted to take me there themselves. Justin went with Jude, Lucas and Fran. We left in convoy, and as we did we saw Lou standing by the roadside without his new bride.

He waved and blew me a kiss. I reciprocated.

This was the new Annabel. That slice of life was behind me and I was off to get me a new slice!

As we headed towards Manchester Airport, I went over the past few months in my head.

How had I turned up at a random caravan park on the outskirts of a Nottinghamshire village to find myself on my way to the airport to start a PA job on the other side of the world? Life can be so sweet sometimes.

'So are you ready to start work in a couple of weeks, chutney?' My dad sounded so excited for me.

'Yeah, I can't wait now, Dad. I feel like a kid in a candy shop! I'm so excited about seeing the sights and I'll have my own place. I've never had my own place.'

'What about the campervan? Or should we say weeping willow van?' he said.

We all started laughing at my grand attempt to make campervan living normal.

'Yeah, well that wasn't quite my own place. It was just a stopgap till someone snapped me up for better things. I knew working for Lieutenant Morris was the best thing I'd ever done, even though he stank of BO and drank like a fish, thinking no one else knew.'

I rolled my eyes at Mum.

'I remember you working there. It was probably the most we had ever heard from you as you had a phone on your desk. As soon as your boss popped out, you rang us... a lot!' She smiled at me and grabbed my hand.

'Please make that a habit again,' she continued. 'You've only rung us once a week or so since you've been at Sunnyside. We've been so worried about you, but we didn't want to interfere. Anyway, I'm pleased we didn't because it all seems to have worked out for you at last.' She gave my hand another squeeze.

I started to see signs for the airport and began to feel nervous and excited all at once.

'Here we are, chutney,' Dad said, stating the obvious. I had kind of figured that out as a huge plane was flying over us, ready to land.

'What time's the flight?' Mum asked.

She never listened, so we always had to tell her everything a hundred times.

'Ten thirty. It's a night flight. We have to change in Dubai and then Bangkok. We'll be there by Christmas!' I said this half in jest and half in the knowledge that it really was going to take ages.

We parked the car and Dad insisted on dragging my case, as if I was an evacuee being sent abroad to live with another family. I could tell they were nervous about me going as they were being far too polite and quiet.

'Hey, I'm not going away forever. It'll be Christmas soon and Lucas has already said he'll pay for my flight back. Come on, that's only a couple of months away. It's no different from when I was in the navy. I couldn't even make it home at Christmas then, 'cause I was at sea somewhere.'

I grabbed each of their arms on the nearest side to me and we linked as we walked. That seemed to perk them up a bit.

I walked towards the check-in desk and saw Justin standing there. I waved and he nodded back as he tried to concentrate on the questions he was being asked by the lady behind the desk.

By the time it was my turn, I noticed Justin was in the business class queue and he was nodding for me to join it.

No way, I thought. *I'll be turning right on the flight, not left!*

We congregated in the departures hall and made small talk. Lucas had sent out emails so everyone would know when we would be landing and where we would be staying.

Everything seemed to be under control. Fran and Jude appeared to be sharing a private joke as they were giggling away behind clasped hands. It was nice to see them chatting and laughing with one another again.

'Can all passengers on flight VS167 to Dubai please get ready to board? Business class and those who need assistance, please board first,' a very camp voice rang out over the tannoy.

Those things always made people talk in the strangest way.

"That's us then, Bella. Let's do this, girl.' Justin took my hand in a gentlemanly way.

I turned to my parents and hugged them tight. 'I love you, and thanks for being my rock. I'll be in touch from all the airports and will call you loads when I get there.'

A tear ran down my cheek and Mum wiped it away.

'Tears of happiness I will simply wipe away; tears of sadness I will wipe away before finding out who made my finger wet,' she said, hugging me tight. 'Go get 'em, Bella baby.'

'Love you, chutney. Stay safe and ring your mother… and me…. lots!' Dad kissed both my cheeks and then gave me hug. 'You make us so proud,' he whispered in my ear.

'Bye, everyone, we'll be in touch,' said Justin. 'Mr McClintock, please don't worry about Bella. She's finally making life happen.'

It was cheesy, but Dad seemed to like it.

I blew my folks a kiss and was dragged towards the gates by Justin. I couldn't keep my eyes off my mum, but she nodded and waved, mouthing, 'It's all good' as she did so. Coming from my mum, this made me feel at ease. I took one last look at them and knew I had made the right decision.

We showed the cabin crew our tickets and turned left to be shown to our posh seats. We stowed our hand luggage away, sat down and sighed. Then we looked at each other and giggled.

'So, Bella, is this your first time in business class?' Justin asked sarcastically, noting the pure glee on my face.

'What do you think?'

'Well, the toilets are loads bigger than in economy, you know.' He winked at me.

'Oi! Not on your nelly!' I hit him with a cushion.

'Champagne?' he asked.

'Yeah, why not?' I rested my head back and looked out of the porthole at a grey, rainy Manchester.

Yes, champagne all the way, because I am Annabel McClintock, and this is the start of a new slice of life!

The next book follows the story of Annabel's adventures in Singapore.

Printed in Great Britain
by Amazon

81916264R00113